THE EMPEROR'S CURSE

CARYN MCCANN

Book Cover by Nabin Karna

ISBN: 979-8-9932858-0-1 (Paperback)

ISBN: 979-8-9932858-1-8 (E-Book)

Want behind-the-scenes intel, deleted scenes, and news about upcoming releases? Join the insider list at CarynMcCann.com for exclusive reveals and surprises!

To my wonderful husband Tom. Thank you for believing in me.

Contents

Chapter 1

The foothills of Coloma, California, birthplace of the Gold Rush, lay quiet in the early morning haze. The wind stirred the grass lining the trail. A worn path cut across the slope toward a rocky hill, where the entrance to an old mine sat like a gaping mouth. It was half hidden by brush, its timbers rotting, forgotten by time.

Chief Jones, an African American man in his late fifties, stepped out of his dusty sedan. No jacket. Just a shirt and tie and the weight of the department on his shoulders. He crossed the overlook and found Officer Garcia, sturdy and sharp-eyed, standing beside yellow tape fluttering between two oak branches.

Jones followed Garcia's gaze to a nervous teenage boy sitting on a rock nearby, arms wrapped around his knees.

"The kid found him this morning?" Jones asked.

"Scott Lee. Son of Old Man Lee, the guy with the dry cleaner back in Folsom," Garcia said. "Claims he came up here hiking. Alone. Trail's been closed since last week's once-in-a-century storm, but he blew past the signs anyway. Found a body half-buried outside the shaft."

Jones squinted down at the mine entrance. "And the body?"

"Badly decayed. My guess? Been here decades."

Dr. Shepherd, a pathologist from UC Davis Medical Center, approached from the dig site with a glint of curiosity in his eyes. Rumpled sport coat. Intensity behind the wire-rimmed glasses.

"The body's at least 150 years old," he said, extending a weathered hand. "Chief Jones, I presume?"

Jones shook it firmly. "That's right. Appreciate you coming out, Dr. Shepherd. But how'd you beat us here?"

"We've been on-site for hours," Dr. Shepherd said, smiling. "Your young witness didn't call the station. He called my protégé, Yu-Chen Huang. I believe you've met."

A few yards from the collapsed shaft, Yu-Chen, a methodical researcher in his early thirties, crouched beside a weathered knapsack. Wearing latex gloves, he sorted through the contents, eyes sharp with curiosity.

"We got a little caught up in the excitement," Shepherd admitted. "You know how it is—an untouched site like this? Hard to resist."

Jones folded his arms. "Doctor, this is a police matter. I appreciate your enthusiasm, but next time, the call should come from us—not the other way—"

Yu-Chen called out, "Dr. Shepherd—I found something!"

Garcia and Jones followed the voice to the tarp-covered body. Yu-Chen stood, energized. "Oh! Chief Jones. Didn't hear your car."

Jones gave a nod. "Garcia says the hiker contacted you directly. Why?"

"Scott Lee. I know his dad. Said the kid was having a rough time at home, needed someone to talk to. I took him hiking out here a while back. Before the rains. Guess he wanted to come back and explore on his own."

Jones gestured to the tarp. "And who do we have?"

Yu-Chen held up an old identity card, edges curled with age. "He had an identity card on him. His name's Li Zhong."

"Yu-Chen this is wonderful! We have a name, and with DNA analysis we can pinpoint where he came from. Excellent news!" said Dr. Shepherd.

"Lucky break," Garcia muttered.

Yu-Chen added, "After the Chinese Exclusion Act in 1882, Chinese immigrants had to carry these papers or risk deportation."

Garcia raised a brow. "That was already a law back then?"

Yu-Chen nodded. "Yeah. California was flooded with Chinese laborers chasing gold. The lucky ones didn't mine, They sold tools, supplies, food. Some made enough to go back home wealthy."

Jones looked down at the body. "But this guy didn't make it back."

"Maybe he wasn't planning to," Garcia said. "Could've left more than just poverty behind. Men don't vanish across the ocean unless they've got something to run from."

Jones gave a slow nod, eyes still on the corpse. "Maybe so." He turned to the pathologist. "Dr. Shepherd, what's the status?"

Dr. Shepherd peeled back the tarp. "Young adult male, maybe late thirties at death. We won't know more until the lab but based on the date of the identity card, you're looking at a body that's been here since the late 1800s."

Dr. Shepherd replaced the sheet and stood. "This could be a major find," Shepherd added, his voice electric. "State funding. Museum interest. We might be looking at a preserved chapter of gold rush history."

"Find any gold?" Garcia joked.

Yu-Chen chuckled. "No, but I haven't checked his—"

The hum of tires cut through the hillside stillness.

A black sedan and a matching van sped up the dirt path, both flying small Chinese flags on their hoods. The engines were still ticking when four men stepped out. They wore sharp suits, dark glasses, and expressions that didn't invite questions.

One wore a tailored coat and a calm, controlled expression—Agent Bao Ming.

Garcia stiffened. "Who the hell are they?"

Jones's gaze locked on the miniature Chinese flags fluttering on the hoods. "Mainland officials, by the look of it."

Garcia glanced back at the vehicles, unsettled. "Over a body? How the hell did they find out so fast?"

"Anything on the wire can get flagged. International monitors sweep for key terms."

Garcia snorted. "With all due respect, Chief, Folsom PD isn't exactly global news."

Jones didn't flinch. "Maybe we are today."

Ming approached, handing Jones a card. "I am Agent Bao Ming. Chinese Ministry of State Security. We were notified of a body—possibly a Chinese national—discovered here."

Jones said, "News travels fast."

As Jones studied the card, Ming loosened his collar, pulling out a midnight-blue pack of HaoMao cigarettes. He slid one out but paused, meeting the chief's stern glare. Ming tucked the pack away, expression unchanged, but Yu-Chen clocked the brand. HaoMao was rare outside Shaanxi province.

"We'll be taking custody of the remains and associated artifacts," Ming said without waiting.

Dr. Shepherd stepped forward. "Not so fast. I'm Dr. Shepherd with UC Davis. I've got jurisdiction to evaluate this body. A business card isn't sufficient authority to seize historical remains."

Ming's voice was smooth, controlled. "Some individuals fled China to avoid prosecution. Their crimes don't expire with time. That's all I'm authorized to say. If you have concerns, I suggest contacting your State Department."

Garcia scoffed. "You're chasing fugitives from two centuries ago? Remind me never to jaywalk in Beijing."

"Officer Garcia," Jones said.

He turned back to Ming, attempting to reassert some control. "Agent Ming, there's no need to escalate this. But if you're requesting custody of human remains, I'll need formal documentation. Something I can file."

Ming said, "Of course." He glanced at his watch, cuff lifting just enough for Yu-Chen to glimpse the edge of a dragon tattoo swirling above the wrist—striking, unnatural on an official.

Jones's phone rang.

"You should take that," Ming said, already turning toward his men.

Jones hesitated, then answered. "Chief Jones... Governor Gaffney—yes, I'm here with Agent Ming now." His eyes flicked toward Ming, narrowing. He took a few steps away, voice quiet but tense. The call lasted less than thirty seconds.

When Jones returned, his expression had hardened into something unreadable.

Ming was already waiting.

"You work fast."

Ming gave a nod.

"My men will take over now," Ming said. "Dr. Shepherd. Please leave everything."

Reluctantly, Yu-Chen placed the identity card near the tarp.

Shepherd leaned in. "You still have the knapsack?"

Yu-Chen hesitated. "Yes, but—"

"Slip it into your bag."

Yu-Chen glanced toward Ming and his men, then tucked the weathered knapsack closer to his leg.

The four Chinese agents clustered nearby, whispering in Mandarin. One held up the identity card. They recognized the name. Their voices rose, urgent and excited.

Yu-Chen's pulse kicked. He shoved the knapsack toward his backpack, but his gloved fingers struck something solid. Nestled among the cloth was a small clay vial, cool and smooth.

He hesitated. Yu-Chen risked a glance inside. The clay vial held several ounces of gold dust—dense in weight, but dancing like vapor. The particles hovered in slow spirals, moved by no force he could name. Not wind. Not gravity. Something else.

He looked up. Ming and the other agents were only feet away.

Yu-Chen slipped the vial back into the knapsack and shoved everything deep into his backpack, sealing it shut as his heart thundered.

Yu-Chen and Dr. Shepherd backed away from the commotion. The hillside wind picked up again, rustling the trees above the mine. The gold was no longer buried. But its danger was just beginning.

Yu-Chen's backpack felt heavier than it should.

He didn't look back.

Chapter 2

Mike White's massive frame filled the cramped motel room as he paced. Each step sent vibrations through the paper-thin walls. The air hung thick with the lingering scent of cheap perfume and sweat—two hours of trying to forget his problems in a stranger's arms, only to create a nightmare far worse.

He couldn't look at the bed. Couldn't look at her pale skin against those stained sheets, couldn't meet those vacant eyes that seemed to follow his movement around the room. The neon VACANCY sign outside cast everything in sickly pink intervals—light, dark, light, dark—like a dying heartbeat.

Murder. The word hammered in his skull with each heavy footstep. That's what any judge would call it. But he'd driven all the way from Folsom to San Francisco precisely to avoid judges, questions, the prying eyes of a town where everyone knew Mike White as the dependable guy who never caused trouble.

Until tonight.

An engine growled in the night, smooth and powerful. The sound crushed the weak clatter of junkers in the lot. Mike's skin prickled. He pulled the curtain aside, eyes narrowing as a sleek Bentley rolled in, headlights slicing through the gloom.

Relief hit first. Then the familiar knot of dread.

Before the man could knock, Mike yanked open the door. Hyde filled the frame, silver hair immaculate, moving with the unhurried confidence of a man who always owned the room.

A second figure followed him in. He was tall, broad-shouldered, his head shaved to a clean shine. The dark blazer fit like body armor. He moved without a hint of wasted motion, eyes combing the small, shabby room with a soldier's discipline and a predator's patience.

Snake didn't offer a hand. He shut the door, crossed to the corner, and leaned into the shadows—silent, steady, watching. His kind of silence carried weight. It pressed on Mike's throat before a word was spoken.

"I must say, Michael," Hyde said, voice smooth as glass, "next time you crave San Francisco's nightlife, a little notice would be appreciated. I walked away from a poker table tonight, and Henderson was already three cards into losing ten grand."

Mike's gaze kept straying to the man by the door.

Hyde caught the look, a hint of amusement on his face. "That's Snake. My driver," he said. "He handles more than the car."

Snake didn't look at the body. His eyes moved once over the room, then settled on Mike, steady and unreadable. The kind of look that made a man reconsider breathing too loud.

Mike forced his jaw to unclench. "Can we just get this done? I need to be back in Folsom in a few hours, and—"

"Don't." Hyde's voice dropped to a whisper sharp enough to cut. "Don't tell me how to practice my craft."

He set his leather medical bag on the cigarette-scarred dresser. The brass clasps clicked open—sharp, deliberate. "Now then, there's the matter of my fee."

Mike's voice cracked. "How much?"

Hyde's smile was almost kind, but his eyes weren't. "Oh, Michael... you couldn't count that high if you had all night."

As they spoke, Snake hadn't moved. But Mike could feel the man's stillness like pressure on his skin, a silent reminder that Hyde never walked into a problem without backup.

Hyde drew a syringe from the bag, the metal catching the sickly light from the ceiling fixture. "Tell me, was she left-handed or right-handed?"

"I don't know. I don't know anything about her except—" Mike swallowed hard. "I just needed... I paid her, that's all. Two hundred for the night."

Hyde tugged her wrist into place. The shift turned her arm just enough for the bracelet to flare. Five stones traced the chain, bright against the pale skin, but the center gem dominated the rest. It was an oval sapphire, darker, deeper, pulling the light toward it while the smaller stones only echoed its shine.

Mike's chest tightened. He'd seen cheap glass sparkle on back-alley wrists, but this wasn't fake. Nobody wore something like that without backing. Dealer's gift, stolen trophy, maybe a boyfriend with muscle. Whatever its story, it didn't belong here.

"Of course you did." Hyde set the needle with precision, sliding it home in one clean motion. "Anonymous transactions are very wise. No emotional complications."

When he closed the bag, his sleeve slipped. From his cuff, a sapphire gleamed—oval, dark, the same cut, the same weight as the one on her bracelet.

For a moment Mike felt pinned, caught between the dead girl's wrist and Hyde's hand—two stones staring back at him, reflecting a secret he wasn't meant to see.

Hyde smoothed the sapphire cufflink at his wrist until it caught the light. "Strange, isn't it? Men ruin themselves faster on cheap appetites than expensive ones."

Mike's eyes darted to the bruises circling her throat. "What about—"

"The bruising?" Hyde's smile turned to a thin line. "Occupational hazard in her line of work. These things happen."

"It was an accident!" The words burst out of Mike. "She asked for it rough!"

"Of course." Hyde snapped the case of the syringe shut. "By the time she's found, the story will speak for itself. And no one at the coroner's office is going to waste time on an overdose from this part of town."

Hyde fastened his bag. "As for my fee... let's call this one on the house. An investment in our future. But do get yourself tested, Michael. One can never be too careful."

Snake opened the door with quiet efficiency. Early dawn light bled into the sleezy room. Hyde walked out first; Snake waited three heartbeats, his eyes never leaving Mike's, before following.

From the window, Mike watched Snake drive Hyde away. Mike realized the Bentley was just out of view of the lobby's security camera. The camera caught every detail of Mike's rental car—enough to trace straight back to Folsom.

His phone vibrated. The favor you owe me will be collected soon. Delete this message. —DH

Mike's palms were damp as he read it. Outside, the taillights vanished into the waking city. Snake's wordless stare still lingered in Mike's head.

Hyde hadn't helped him out of kindness. And now there was more than one set of hands pulling his strings.

Chapter 3

One year later

Saturday morning. The American Gold Rush Museum was closed, a temporary closure sign taped to the glass entrance. The museum's director, an African American man, Marcus Washington, looked perplexed as Officer Paige Gold interviewed him. Paige — a sharp-eyed, no-nonsense cop in her early 30s with a warrior's bearing, shoulder-length brown hair, and hazel eyes that don't miss much — checked her notepad.

She stepped onto the creaky wood floor, the scent of dust and aged pine lingering in the air. Rows of exhibit cases glowed under soft yellow spotlights, throwing shadows across old tools, gold pans, and faded canvas gear. A life-sized mannequin in a red plaid shirt stood frozen mid-scoop beside a tin pan filled with gravel, like a miner caught in time.

"Nothing but a few pairs of miners' jeans? Nothing else was stolen?" Paige asked as she eyed the high-arched sign near the entrance that read *HO! CALIFORNIA*—the unofficial anthem of 1849 fortune hunters.

The museum director huffed. "I've been over these displays ten times. Thankfully, nothing else was taken. They didn't even touch the garnets on loan from the El Dorado County Museum. The thief couldn't have been that smart."

Paige glanced toward the far wall, where a small dome-shaped security camera hung lifeless above the glass case. "Well, they cut the CCTV feed before they broke in. That takes planning." She flipped a page in her notebook. "Was there anything of value inside the miner's clothing display? Anything worth more than nostalgia?"

Marcus snorted, gesturing toward the now empty display case behind the mannequin. "No gold nuggets, if that's what you're thinking. Just a few original Levi's—worn, patched, dusty. Valuable to collectors, maybe. But not worth breaking into a museum over."

A faint hum came from the overhead lights, broken only by the occasional creak from the floorboards. Paige stepped closer to the case, noting the clean pry marks at the base. They looked precise, practiced. Whoever took the jeans hadn't been in a rush.

"We'll be in touch. Thank you, Mr. Washington".

Paige walked over to her partner, Officer Mike White, a uniformed cop with a habit of charging ahead before asking questions. Lately, she'd started to wonder what he might be keeping to himself. He was inspecting the CCTV camera mounted on the wall.

"Any luck on the camera, Mike?" Paige asked.

Officer White didn't look up right away. "The feed was cut over two days ago. Marcus probably forgot to pay his security bill."

Something in his tone was too casual, too dismissive. Paige studied him as he rubbed the back of his neck—his tell when he was avoiding something.

"I'll start canvassing the neighborhood," she said. "See if anyone spotted something last night."

"No." He straightened. "Don't waste police resources. You need to review the rest of the CCTV footage back at the station. File the report—"

"So you want to bury this investigation in red tape, Mike?"

His jaw clenched. “No canvassing. Garcia will handle it tonight.”

Paige blinked. “Mike, the first few hours are key. I’ll cover Main Street—”

“I gave you an order, and you’re refusing to follow it. You want me to put that in writing?”

His voice came out sharp, but he still wouldn’t meet her eyes. Paige frowned. Mike used to be all-in. He'd charge into scenes, push for leads. Now his shoulders were tense, eyes calculating.

“Now get the damn tapes from Marcus’s office. We’re done here,” White snapped, already turning to leave.

Paige crossed her arms. “Mike, the feed’s been down for two days. You know the tapes won’t show anything.”

He didn’t look back. “Doesn’t matter. Grab them anyway. We’ll log the case and move on.”

She stepped in front of him. “So, we’re closing this out with no suspects, no leads, and stolen artifacts we can’t explain?”

White finally met her eyes. But his stare was flat, guarded. “It’s a couple pairs of old jeans, Paige. Let it go.”

Her jaw tightened. “You sure that’s all it is?”

A beat. He held her gaze, unmoving. Then blinked. “Get the tapes.”

He turned and stormed off, boots heavy on the polished floorboards.

Paige watched him go, the air thick with something unsaid. Her gut tightened. Mike was hiding something. And whatever it was, it started here.

She wandered back toward the old miner display, letting instinct pull her in. One photo drew her attention. It was an 1850s image of a weary Chinese man crouched beside a washtub, laundry sloshing in a battered bucket. Behind him stood a crooked cabin, and a hand-painted sign: Free Washing & Laundry.

Several white miners stood beside him, lined up like customers. Paige leaned in, eyes narrowing at the faded placard. Her gut stirred. He wasn't just doing laundry. He was washing *jeans.*

"Who's this guy?" she asked.

Marcus appeared beside her, his voice smooth, respectful. "Locals called him John-John. Back then, white folks used the same nickname for every Chinese man. His real name is lost to history."

Paige raised an eyebrow. "He really washed miners' clothes for free?"

"That's the legend," Marcus said. "He figured out that the gold dust caught in the seams of their pants was worth more than anything they'd pay him. So, he offered his services for free, and they thought he was a fool." He smiled. "Turns out, he was the smartest man in the room."

Paige stared at the old denim in the photo. The jeans. The washtub. The sign. "Maybe that's why someone stole them," she said, half-joking. "Thought they could shake out a few flakes of 175-year-old gold dust."

Marcus gave a soft laugh. "If that was the plan, they left disappointed. All our artifacts are screened and cleaned before they go on display."

She nodded but kept staring. *Still... why jeans? Why now?*

"Why break into a museum," she murmured, "when you can buy gold on the open market without risking jail?"

Marcus crossed his arms, thoughtful. "Maybe they weren't after gold."

Then, with a glance back at the photo: "Or maybe they believe anything buried for 175 years carries something more. Rarity has a pull all its own."

Paige tilted her head. "Gold fever never really dies, huh?"

Marcus smiled. "Not around here."

A silence settled between them—thoughtful, uneasy. Outside, the summer sun dipped behind the hills, casting long shadows across the museum's scuffed hardwood floor.

Paige's gaze drifted to her notes. *Black Core Labs.* The name had come up in Marcus's funding records. Strange backing for a small-town museum. She circled it, making a mental note to ask Yu-Chen. He seemed to know something about every biotech player in the region.

Paige glanced at the empty display case—her mind drifting for just a second. Months earlier, she and Yu-Chen had wandered this same room. He'd paused at the jeans display, tapping the glass, the ghost of a grin on his lips. "Gold dust changed lives, but it also ruined them," he'd said softly. "Most miners chasing it ended up broke or worse. What's precious can be a curse too." Then, grinning, "If you ever see me get greedy, remind me of these jeans." It was easy with Yu-Chen—honest, uncomplicated, nothing like her time with David. With David, every day was a negotiation, an argument over commitment or calendars. With Yu-Chen, she could simply… coast. She blinked, the memory fading, and flipped to a fresh page.

Something about this didn't sit right. And her gut told her it was just the beginning.

Chapter 4

Yu-Chen Huang hunched over his laptop, the bluish LED seemed to shift the shadows beneath his eyes from tired to haunted. The lab was never truly quiet—machines murmured and clicked, refrigerators rasped in slow cycles. But Yu-Chen had long ago tuned his senses to the rhythms of sleepless science.

Rows of glass flasks shimmered gold under the overhead lights, looking almost precious—a hundred possible futures distilled in honeyed liquid.

He'd always been the silent one in every lab, the observer tucked at the edge of a room: sharp-eyed, patient, never needing to speak first or loudest. He wasn't striking. His jaw uncertain, his face always half-lit by a monitor. But his intensity, the way he noticed small things and filed them away, had a gravity all its own. Yu-Chen saw what others missed. And he never forgot, not when it mattered.

During the week, he lived in the data wings of UC Davis Medical Center, buried in clinical trials and tissue samples. But come Friday night, he returned to Folsom and vanished into the basement of Black Core Labs like Superman ducking into a phone booth. This place, this windowless lab, was where he dreamed bigger—ending world hunger. Saving lives.

A knock.

Three deliberate taps. Calm. Measured.

Yu-Chen turned. Behind the glass stood Doctor Hyde—tall, crisp in a tailored suit, early fifties. There was nothing hurried about him. His coat was pressed. His posture precise. The kind of man who never had to raise his voice because control followed him in silence.

Yu-Chen buzzed him in.

"Doctor Hyde. I wasn't expecting you."

Hyde entered without comment or hesitation, his gaze scanning the lab like he was inspecting property. Because, in a way, he was.

"I'm glad you keep it locked," he said, his voice smooth. "Be a shame if your miracle compound disappeared into someone else's hands. Corporate theft is such a nuisance. And I've invested a great deal."

His eyes lingered on the flask glowing gold inside its heated coil, then drifted to the open notebook near Yu-Chen's elbow.

Yu-Chen slid it toward the edge of the bench. But Hyde's eyes were already moving—slow, calculated.

"Still working both jobs," Hyde said, circling. "Clinical Research Fellow by day, miracle worker by night. I do worry about your health, Yu-Chen."

"I'm fine," Yu-Chen replied, voice even. "Weekends are quiet. I use them well."

"I think it's time you reconsider your priorities. That so-called miracle cure of yours? *That* is the future. Not UC Davis Medical Center. Not your day job. This."

He nodded to the lab bench.

"This is what matters."

"I'm already putting in full-time hours here."

"That's not what I mean."

Hyde stepped closer, eyes on Yu-Chen.

"Perhaps it's time we revisit the terms of our partnership."

Yu-Chen held his gaze. "I'm listening."

As Hyde drifted closer, Yu-Chen slid the notebook into the bottom drawer, careful not to let the page marked "Three doses remaining" catch Hyde's eye. Hyde probably knew. He always seemed to.

Without breaking eye contact, he eased it into the bottom drawer and closed it with a soft click.

If Hyde noticed, he gave no sign.

"I think we can agree," Hyde said, circling the bench again, "that without my backing, this little experiment of yours, this so-called miracle compound, would still be collecting dust in a university fridge." He glanced over, a smile tugging at his mouth, cool and amused. "What are you calling it again? Project Regenesis?"

Yu-Chen nodded once. "You funded it. Access to your lab accelerated the work. I've never denied that."

"And yet," Hyde said, stepping to the edge of the table, "you still haven't delivered anything. No working sample. No proof it does more than make a houseplant perk up."

"It's not ready."

"You said it could revive dead matter."

"I said it showed promise. In plants."

Hyde's voice cooled. "With all the capital I've invested, I believe I'm owed more than 'promise.' I want a sample."

Yu-Chen's jaw clenched. "That's not in the contract."

"No. But the contract does say I can pull out. I can take everything if there's no deliverable within twelve months. We're at thirteen, aren't we?"

"You'd kill the golden goose? That's not like you."

"On the contrary. I know exactly what I'm doing."

Hyde stepped even closer, the faint scent of his cologne—something sterile, chemical—catching in Yu-Chen's throat.

"There's a path forward," Hyde said. "We revise the contract. Expand the trials to human subjects. I already have access to willing participants."

Yu-Chen unfolded a crumpled flyer and slid it across the bench.

WANTED: Volunteers for New Drug Study.
We pay $$$! No risk. Cure disease today! Call 555-1212.

"Willing?" he said. "Or just desperate? One of the clinic's volunteers found this taped outside the soup kitchen. The number leads straight to your Black Core testing facility."

Hyde's smile twitched.

"Don't even think about testing your bootleg copy on people," Yu-Chen snapped. "You don't have my formula. And you never will. This was never meant for human trials. It's designed to restore dead plant tissue, to fight food shortages. Not fuel your ambition."

Hyde straightened, voice harder now. "You talk about reviving plants, ending food shortages, curing starvation. But why stop there?" He took another step forward. "Cancer. Neurodegeneration. We could solve all of it. With my reach and your formula, we could change the world. All we need is a few human trials."

Yu-Chen didn't blink. "You cannot use my compound on people. It's unstable. Dangerous. If I hear you've tested it on even one person, the partnership is over."

Hyde's voice dropped, cold as steel. "You don't have that option."

He moved in, slow and quiet, never raising his voice.

"I own your debt. This lab. Your equipment. I could bury you so deep in litigation, you'd be lucky to draw blood at a strip mall vet clinic."

Then came the cold smile.

"I'll expect a sample by next week."

His hand touched the door, but he glanced back one last time.

"And Yu-Chen, if you so much as whisper about ending this, my legal team will freeze your assets and confiscate everything. Your data. Your equipment. All three remaining lots of your precious *Project Regenesis.*"

He lingered on the name with mocking care.

"I've already spoken to marketing. We'll be calling it *Lifegold.* Catchy, don't you think? Test groups loved it."

The door clicked shut behind him.

Yu-Chen stood still, staring at the closed drawer. Hyde had seen it. Knew exactly what it contained.

Only three doses of the mysterious gold dust left.

Breath tight, he gripped the edge of the table, eyes locked on the drawer.

Project Regenesis was never about branding.

It was about saving lives.

He had to get out from under Hyde's control. Now. The three vials were his last defense against Hyde, against his own ambition, maybe against the world. If Hyde got them, it was over. Not just for Yu-Chen. For Paige. For anyone foolish enough to trust miracles.

Chapter 5

Paige stepped out of the Gold Rush Museum and into the light. Sutter Street unfurled ahead of her. False-front buildings with hand-painted signs had the worn charm of a town trying to preserve its past. The pan-for-gold tourist sign tilted like it had been waiting all week for someone to fix it.

She glanced toward the storefronts. "Mike, why are you so against me canvassing for witnesses?"

Officer White pulled out his phone. "Garcia will handle it."

"Garcia's on nights. You think he's gonna find a shop owner who'll talk after six?"

White scoffed. "We're talking about a pair of antique jeans, Paige. Let's not act like it's a homicide."

Ahead, a familiar figure sat on a bench near a shuttered candy shop. Old Charlie was a lean, lined Chinese man in his seventies. He held his cap in both hands. A folded cardboard sign rested beside him. A woman passed, her bag swinging at her hip.

"Excuse me, ma'am," Charlie said. "Spare a dollar so I can buy some lunch?"

The woman picked up her pace and raised a tissue to her face as Charlie broke into a cough that sounded like it had been building all week.

White shook his head. "You want to help someone? Get that Chinaman off the street and into the shelter."

Paige turned. "His name is Charlie. And you know he won't go."

"Make him." White was already veering off toward the baby-blue coffee truck down the block. "I need caffeine."

Paige let out a breath through her nose and spotted Sam, the sandwich vendor, sliding a cooler into the back of a small office. She crossed the street.

"Hey, Sam. Got any turkey left?"

Sam looked up, his eyes lighting. "Officer Paige. Early lunch?"

"Still on duty. Lunch is two hours away." She pulled a few bills from her pocket.

"No hummus and veggie today?" Sam asked. "That's a first."

"It's not for me."

She crossed the street, sandwich in hand, and spotted Charlie near his usual bench, working the sidewalk with that half-toothless grin that disarmed more than a few pedestrians. His eyes lit up when he saw her.

"Well, look who it is," he said, grinning. "My favorite badge-wearin' beauty."

"You know panhandling's not allowed," Paige said. He held up both hands, palms open. "Oh, it's not for me. I'm collecting for the Hungry Ghosts."

She squinted at him. "The what now?"

"It's the last week of the Hungry Ghost Festival. Gotta buy food and leave it out for the departed, or they'll think we've forgotten them."

Paige snorted. "Sounds like a total waste to me."

Charlie's grin faded just a little. "It's not a waste. Families put out offerings, and after the spirits pass through, they can eat it themselves. It's—"

"Charlie," she cut in, "enough with the Chinese culture lesson."

She sat beside him, held out the sandwich. "Eat. This is for you. Not some ghost with an appetite."

Charlie accepted it like she'd handed him gold. "Turkey, huh? You sure know how to spoil a man." He sat down on the bench and unwrapped the sandwich.

"Come on. Let me take you to the shelter. You look like you haven't seen a mattress in a week."

Charlie eased back against the bench, exhaling like it took effort. "Nah. I like sleeping under the stars. No lights, no snoring, no curfew. Freedom, Officer Paige, and the price is right."

A wet, rattling cough tore through Charlie's chest. Paige winced. He sounded worse than last week.

She'd been checking on Charlie for almost two years now—ever since she'd found him passed out behind the hardware store during her first month on patrol. Most cops would have just called it in, but something about his dignity, even in that moment, had gotten to her. Maybe it was the way he'd apologized for the trouble, or how he'd carefully folded his cardboard sign before the paramedics arrived.

Their routine had developed slowly: she'd swing by his usual spots, bring him food when she could, try to talk him into the shelter when the weather turned. He'd tell her stories about his better days. Stories about working construction, his late wife, and the grandson who'd stopped calling. She never pushed too hard. Charlie was proud, and pride was sometimes all a person had left.

But this cough was new. And worse.

"You're not bulletproof, Charlie. You look like hell. Just crash at the shelter tonight. Promise me that."

He gave her a crooked grin, eyes a little too glassy beneath the grime and fatigue. "No need to worry, Officer Paige. I won't be out here much longer."

She frowned. "Oh yeah? Why's that?"

"Landed a gig," he said, tapping his chest with quiet pride. "Some kinda research program. Said I'd be part of something cutting-edge."

He held up a cheap black phone and wiggled it between two fingers. "Came with perks. Even got me a shiny new burner."

Paige narrowed her eyes. The phone was generic. No case, no branding. Screen already cracked. Something about it itched at her instincts.

"Who's 'they'?"

Charlie tapped the side of his nose. "All very hush-hush. Medical-sounding folks. I saw their flyer tacked up at the soup kitchen. Said they were looking for volunteers."

He gave a vague shrug. "Some health thing. Paid gig. Said I was perfect for it."

Perfect for it. Paige didn't like the sound of that.

In her experience, when researchers called homeless people "perfect" for anything, it usually meant they were desperate enough not to ask questions. Charlie was smart. He was smarter than his circumstances suggested, but he was also vulnerable. And someone was clearly taking advantage of that.

She felt the familiar tug of wanting to protect him, the same instinct that made her bring sandwiches instead of citations. Charlie reminded her of her grandfather somehow—stubborn, independent, too proud to accept help even when he needed it most.

"Did they give you any paperwork?"

"Nah. Just the phone. Said instructions would come later. But hey, it's a golden opportunity, right?"

Paige studied his face, noting the hope flickering beneath the bravado. Charlie wanted this to be real. He wanted to believe someone saw value in him beyond spare change and pity. The thought of crushing that hope made her chest tight, but every cop instinct she had was screaming warnings.

He'd unwrapped the sandwich and was already halfway through the first bite.

For a moment, she just watched him eat—the careful way he savored each bite, making it last. It was a reminder of how different their worlds were, how what she took for granted could be someone else's highlight of the day.

"Charlie," she said, her voice softer now. "Be careful with this research thing, okay? If anything feels wrong—"

"I know, I know." He waved her off, but his expression had grown serious. "You worry too much, Officer Paige. But I appreciate it. Not many folks would."

She was about to press him for more details about his mysterious gig when her radio crackled to life.

"Unit 2," came desk sergeant Helga's voice, sharp and nasal. "Mrs. Giuseppe says the renters across the street are blasting music again. And tell that slacker Mike to keep his mic on."

Paige lifted the mic. "Copy, base. Unit 2 en route."

Chapter 6

The paper trembled in his hands.

By the dim lamplight of his cottage, Yu-Chen squinted at the fragile Chinese court document he'd smuggled from the UC Medical Center archives. Ink faded. Edges torn. But the words were clear enough.

Li Zhong. Grave robber. Convicted in absentia.

His breath hitched as he reread the passage he'd translated hours ago.

"He opened the resting place of Immortal Zhou, a Taoist alchemist who brewed elixirs for the emperor. Legend says he drank the gold and walked untouched by fire. The robber stole the sacred ash and vanished into the hills."

Yu-Chen exhaled, heart thudding. The gold dust hadn't just come from some geological fluke. It had been stolen from a tomb so feared the locals sealed it for two millennia. They thought the gold dust cursed those who touched it. And now *he* had it.

Dr. Shepherd's warning echoed, like a ghost. *"The less we know, the better."*

Then the image shifted—a sharp curve. Screeching tires on a coastal highway. A shattered guardrail. A sedan crushed nose-first in a ravine. No skid marks. No time to brake.

Brrng. Brrng. Yu-Chen jerked awake at his lab bench, heart pounding, eyes unfocused. His phone vibrated on the counter. He fumbled for it.

"Huang Yu-Chen speaking." His voice was hoarse. A pause. "Ah, Mr. Rosenberg! Thank you for returning my call..."

His spine straightened. "Really? You think there's a way out?"

He listened, eyes coming alive. "Yes, I'll sign the engagement letter tonight. I need to move fast... Got it. Thank you again." He hangs up, pumps his fist.

"Yes!"

He spots a local magazine on a table. The cover shows him shaking hands with Doctor Hyde. With a smirk, he tore the cover from the magazine, crushed it in one hand, and launched it with a mock jump shot. It arced cleanly, landing in the bin with a satisfying *swish.*

Then a knock at the glass lab door. Yu-Chen turns. Behind the glass door stands Mr. Yeung in his seventies, dressed in slacks and a cardigan, holding two takeaway containers. He wears a warm, knowing smile.

Yu-Chen grins and hurries to buzz him in. He meets him at the door.

"Practicing your jump shot, are you?" Mr. Yeung asks, stepping inside. His voice is gentle, amused.

Yu-Chen laughs. "Something like that. I just got some incredible news. Couldn't help myself."

"Your father says you've been working day and night. Not even stopping to eat."

He raises the takeout.

"Figured someone should remind you food exists.

Yu-Chen takes the containers.

"You always know when to show up."

The two men sit at a table.

"Wonton soup. You remembered?"

Mr. Yeung set the containers on the bench and opened one.

"I know it's your favorite. Come, eat before it gets cold."

They sit. Yu-Chen stirs his soup, distracted.

"So..." Mr. Yeung asked, watching him over the rim of his tea. "This incredible news, can you talk about it?"

Yu-Chen hesitated, gaze fixed on the bowl. Steam rose, but he scarcely noticed.

"Actually..." He trailed off, unsure. A dozen easy lies lined up in his mind, but none worth speaking. He'd already told one lie. The one that still made sleep impossible.

Mr. Yeung studied him. After a pause, his voice softened.

"Something troubling you, Yu-Chen?"

Yu-Chen exhaled. Quiet. Measured. He looked up, eyes searching.

"Okay. Here goes. I don't know who else to tell. But I need your advice. You've known me since I was a kid—back when our families lived in Hong Kong. And... you've always been honest with me."

"You can tell me anything, and it stays between us. I won't even tell your dad about our conversation."

"It's Doctor Hyde. My backer. He's now talking about testing my gold dust on humans. It's insane," said Yu-Chen. "Now he's trying to recruit homeless volunteers."

Mr. Yeung's expression darkened. "Testing on homeless people? That's not research, Yu-Chen, that's exploitation. These people are vulnerable, desperate. They can't give true informed consent."

He leaned back, studying Yu-Chen with the calculating look that had made him successful in business for forty years. "But I suspect you already know that. Which makes me wonder. What does Doctor Hyde really want? Because a man doesn't risk his reputation on unethical trials unless the prize is worth it."

Yu-Chen's jaw tightened. "He wants complete control. Of the research, the patents, everything."

"And now?" asked Mr. Yeung.

"Our partnership has gone sour. I needed his backing for my research. But now he's taking too many risks. And he's demanding I hand over the gold dust."

"The gold dust you found last year," said Mr. Yeung. "What makes yours so special that Hyde can't just find his own source?"

"He can't." Yu-Chen leaned in, voice low. "If Hyde tries to fake my discovery, there's a way to prove he's lying. But only I know it."

Mr. Yeung studied him. "Go on."

Yu-Chen shifted, heat prickling the back of his neck. Here we go. The lie he'd rehearsed a hundred times. It wasn't because he wanted to deceive Mr. Yeung, but because the truth would put everyone he cared about in danger.

"After last year's flood, I went exploring in the old Gold Rush caves," he said. "Found fossilized amber with ancient gold particles trapped inside—over a thousand years old. That's what makes it special. Modern gold doesn't work."

Mr. Yeung's gaze sharpened. "Interesting story."

Yu-Chen forced a tight smile, heart hammering. He would die before telling anyone what he'd really found—or where. Some secrets were too dangerous, especially when Chinese agents were still asking questions.

"So, if Doctor Hyde tries to steal my research or cut me out, he'll fail. What I have isn't just raw materials. It's the finished compound. Three doses of the actual cure, refined and ready. Without my process, without knowing the true source, he can't replicate it."

"Your dad said something about making dead grass grow."

"No, that was only my initial tests. It can rejuvenate any dead plant. Think of the possibilities! We could donate it to farmers, export more food to poor communities, even globally!"

"These three doses are just the beginning. I've been analyzing the compound's structure. I think I can synthesize the active components. It'll take time, proper lab work, but it's possible."

Yu-Chen's eyes drifted to the locked drawer. Three vials that could change the world. Or it could destroy his life if anyone learned where the gold dust really came from.

"Doctor Hyde doesn't share your vision?" Mr. Yeung asked.

"He wants to test the compound on people. It's reckless."

"You signed a contract with him?"

"I did. I was desperate. I thought he believed in the science." Yu-Chen shook his head. "Now he's pushing human trials on the homeless. No oversight, no safety protocols. Just exploitation. I've spoken to a lawyer. He thinks there's a way out. So, I'm making two of the biggest decisions of my life this week. One is to end my partnership with Doctor Hyde."

"And the other decision?"

Yu-Chen's eyes sparkle with mischief. He reaches into a drawer and takes out a book. Hands it to Mr. Yeung.

Mr. Yeung notices the title, "*Love: The Ultimate Medicine*. Interesting textbook. Do they teach you about love as medicine in med school now?" Mr. Yeung smiles.

Yu-Chen opens the book to show its hollowed-out interior. Inside is a ring box. He opens the little box.

"It's Paige's engagement ring. Nice, huh?" Yu-Chen said, excited and proud. "My dad loves his bookshop so much, he always says you can find treasure within the pages. So, I literally made it happen."

"Paige Gold. I thought you two had only dated for a few months."

"Almost a year. But we love each other. And why wait? My miracle cure will be a huge success, Doctor Hyde will be out of the picture, and

Paige and I can get married. I can't wait to get this next chapter of my life started."

"Well, congratulations. It just seems a bit...rushed."

"I just got off the phone with a lawyer. I haven't filed anything yet, but I will—immediately. I need out, Mr. Yeung. Hyde's not just a problem anymore—he's a threat."

He drew a breath, steadying himself.

"I was going to wait until our one-year anniversary to propose... but I can't. Not anymore. Everything's moving too fast and not in the right direction. I'm asking Paige on Sunday."

"You mean tomorrow?"

Yu-Chen looked down for a beat, then met Mr. Yeung's eyes.

"I know this seems fast. But I want a clean break—from Hyde, from the lies—before any of it touches her career, or the future I want to build for us."

"But Doctor Hyde owns this lab. He could confiscate everything. Including your mysterious gold dust."

"I thought of that. I'm going to hide the gold dust." Yu-Chen turns the book's spine towards Mr. Yeung and peels back the spine to reveal a second hiding place.

"You're going to give this book with the ring and gold dust to Paige? Shouldn't you wait until you're married before giving her possession of your gold dust? You've got everything riding on your miracle cure."

"My love for Paige knows no bounds. I trust her with my life. I have two other lots of the gold dust. I'll make sure Doctor Hyde won't be able to get his hands on them."

Mr. Yeung looks thoughtful, "I hope you're right about this, Yu-Chen."

Chapter 7

Through the shelves, Yu-Chen saw her slip inside from the bright sidewalk, blinking in the golden September sunlight. Relief and something tighter surged in his chest—time to move.

From the sidewalk, she'd seen the shop glowing with fairy-light warmth, the front windows bustling with people. Inside, the narrow space hummed with the mingled scents of almond cookies, candied orange peel and oolong tea. Tables were piled with books, their titles hidden behind a florist's careful arrangement.

Yu-Chen broke from the crowd, clutching a worn old hardcover like a lifeline. His face was taut but lit with something she couldn't name.

"Sorry! My watch died," she said, cheeks heating.

"You're perfect," he told her, kissing her forehead. He nodded toward his father, Wise Huang, who was laughing with Mrs. Chen and a silver-haired man in the corner, presumably the "visiting author."

Paige took in the scene. The guest list was bigger than she'd expected: local shopkeepers, townsfolk, a few faces she knew from city events. Miguel, her best friend Amy's eager young intern, wove through the crowd snapping candid shots, the big DSLR bouncing on his chest. Amy ran the town's one-woman newspaper, and tonight she'd brought her camera crew of one.

"So... who's the famous author whose schedule magically freed up?" she murmured.

"You'll find out," Yu-Chen said, smiling in that way that made her wary. "Come here."

He drew her toward the signing table. Up close, she noticed the odd detail. Some of the "signing" copies had different titles. Different authors, even. No one was signing anything. The neat display wasn't for a real event at all—it was just for her.

"Yu-Chen, what's going on? Where's the author? And why are there about ten different books on this table?"

"Because today isn't about any of them."

He handed her the battered old book he'd been holding, the title worn nearly to nothing.

"Love Is the Ultimate Medicine?" She gave him a bemused look. "Non-fiction really isn't my—"

"Open it," Yu-Chen said, and when she met his eyes, the earnestness there made her fingers still on the cover.

Inside the hollowed interior was a velvet box. Paige blinked, her heart leaping—half dread, half anticipation.

Yu-Chen dropped to one knee.

"Paige," he said, voice carrying through a hush in the crowd, "I've spent a year chasing discoveries I thought were impossible. But you—" His gaze clung to hers, steady but imploring. "You're the rarest thing I've ever found. Will you marry me?"

A silence. Then: gasps, claps, flashes of Miguel's camera.

Marry him? Paige felt a thousand eyes on her, her pulse thrumming in her ears. She'd wanted love to be simple; lately, every touch reminded her of what she didn't feel. Ever since David, she'd wondered if she'd ever feel that again.

Miguel's camera caught her confusion—half-smiling, teetering between gratitude and guilt.

She tried to anchor herself, reaching for kindness. Yu-Chen was a good man. Wasn't that enough?

"Yes," she whispered at last.

Champagne erupted, laughter burst, and the crowd surged around them. Yu-Chen slipped the ring on her finger, grinning so hard it pained Paige to meet his eyes. Wise Huang and Mrs. Chen congratulated Paige and Yu-Chen. The crowd cheered.

Paige moved through the throng, her thoughts jumbled, her smile automatic. She found herself clutching the engagement ring like a borrowed prop. She barely heard conversations, aware only that she was at the center of something she hadn't fully chosen.

Mr. Yeung drifted near, approving but wary. "Worth its weight in gold," he murmured, nodding to the book she set down on an end table.

Paige smirked. "Don't let Peterson from the antique shop hear you say that. He'd probably offer to buy it on the spot."

Mr. Yeung studied her face, his expression thoughtful. "You seem... unsettled by all this."

Paige's smile faltered slightly. "It's just, everything happened so fast. The proposal, the crowd, all these people watching." She gestured vaguely at the party swirling around them.

"Sudden, perhaps," Mr. Yeung said gently. "But Yu-Chen has the steadiest heart of anyone I know. He doesn't act without certainty."

She tried to reply, but Yu-Chen swept in beside them, animated and radiant. "Come on, let's toast!"

Miguel snapped pictures, Amy directed poses. Paige endured the flash; her eyes watered, but every image was immortalizing her uncertainty, not her joy.

Suddenly, the front door opened. Paige's breath caught.

David Lau stepped in, hesitating at the threshold. His quiet strength filled the space around him, and when his eyes found Paige, she felt a bolt of longing and shame that she couldn't pretend away.

For a fleeting second, she saw something in David: regret, maybe sorrow. Yu-Chen waved him over.

"David! Over here!"

Paige stiffened as David approached. There was no way Yu-Chen missed the sudden tension in the air. It was the kind old friends spotted, and old lovers couldn't hide.

David joined them, smile polite but haunted. "Congratulations, Yu-Chen. Paige."

Paige's voice betrayed her. "You knew?"

Yu-Chen managed a grin, but a shadow flickered in his gaze. "David's been my best friend since med school. Wouldn't let him miss this."

He turned, summoning Mr. Yeung and Wise Huang for a photo—the old family tapestry moment, even as new threads strained at the seams.

While they lined up, Amy arrived with champagne. Paige drank hers in three quick gulps; David accepted the second glass but didn't move closer.

Amy whispered, "Miguel's going to have you on every newsstand."

Paige murmured, "Perfect. Folsom loves a show."

Amy's eyes softened with worry, but before she could say anything, Miguel appeared at her elbow, camera in hand.

"Amy, should I get shots of the cake cutting? And maybe some candids of the families?" Miguel's enthusiasm was infectious, but his timing left something to be desired.

Amy glanced between Paige and David, clearly sensing the tension. "Actually, yes. Get Mr. Huang by the cake table. And see if you can catch Mrs. Chen arranging those cookies. The Chronicle loves those community moments." She squeezed Paige's arm briefly. "We'll talk later, okay?"

As Amy guided Miguel toward the refreshment area, David and Paige were left in their pocket of quiet amid the celebration.

Then, as David waited, Paige said quietly, "You shouldn't have come."

David's reply was gentle. "Yu-Chen made me promise. But I needed to see you."

Her defenses spiked. "It's too late, David."

He hesitated, voice thick. "Paige... do you love him?"

She looked down. The words stuck. "You don't get to ask me that."

David pressed: "Before you say yes for good—"

Before she could answer, a new shadow appeared: Doctor Hyde.

Tall, broad-shouldered, with sharp eyes and a smile that never quite fit, he glided into the circle. "Officer Paige Gold, congratulations. As Yu-Chen's partner, I had to extend my wishes. You've caught quite a prize." His tone was smooth, practiced, layered with meanings she didn't like.

Paige forced herself to stand her ground. "Dr. Hyde, this isn't a time for business."

He extended a red envelope, heavy with cash. His sleeve shifted just enough for a glimpse of sapphire studs at his cuff. Even in the bookshop's soft light, they gleamed, precise and out of place. "A token, Officer Gold. In Chinese tradition, red envelopes mark good fortune."

Paige's fingers stiffened. "This feels like a bribe, not a blessing."

Hyde's smile hardened. "Just a gesture, a partnership. After all, Yu-Chen already accepted my support. And married, you make quite the team." He winked and slipped away.

The red sunset spilled across the shopfront, setting the glass aglow as Hyde slipped through the crowd, jacket crisp, every move practiced. Snake straightened from the shadows near the curb, eyes darting—always scanning, always watching.

"Straight home, sir?" Snake said, ready for duty like muscle memory.

Hyde smirked. "I've been thinking. The Bentley's old news. Meant for men who've already made it. I'm thinking it's time to swap it for the Porsche. Something with bite. Something that says no one's catching up."

Snake hesitated, struggling to hide the nerves behind his jaw. "What about your morning calls—Shanghai, Frankfurt, all that business on the way in? Having me drive saves time."

Hyde laughed softly. "Not interested in being chauffeured anymore, Snake. I miss being king of the road. Why should you have all the fun? Take the night off. Hell, take the whole week."

Snake stiffened as he handed over the car keys. "You didn't hire me just to drive, Doctor Hyde. You know that."

Hyde studied him with that catlike focus, curiosity, calculation, contempt. "Nervous about your contract?"

Snake's reply was quiet, but the hunger was real. "You're on the verge, sir. If Yu-Chen's gold dust pans out, you'll have more than old money. You'll have leverage, power, real fortune. I just don't want to get left out when you change the game."

Snake shook his head, voice harder. "I'm worried about missing my chance. When this hits, you'll have everyone clawing at your door. I've worked the dirt, the risks, all the jobs no one wants. Don't hand the big stuff to White and leave me in the cold."

Hyde paused at the car, measuring Snake's ambition. "So you want more skin in the game?"

Snake didn't flinch. "Give me something real. Not just driving or muscle. Let me earn my cut. I'll make you money, sir—and I'll keep quiet about it."

Hyde flicked the keys. "Expanding your job description means danger, Snake. You know that?"

A flash of a grin. "Danger's where the money is."

Hyde nodded once, getting in. "Tomorrow. Show me you're worth it."

Snake watched as Hyde drove the Bentley away, jaw set. He could practically taste the gold dust—the future, the fortune, the chance he'd kill for.

***

Inside the bookshop, Yu-Chen tapped his glass for a toast. "To my fiancée, Paige Gold—the best thing in my life. And to our future, which looks very bright."

Someone shouted, "Don't forget us when you're rich!"

Yu-Chen laughed. "If Paige wants to keep working, she can. Or maybe she'll retire early!"

Paige's stomach twisted. She met David's gaze across the crowd. They shared a silent exchange layered with questions she wasn't ready to answer.

Miguel's camera flashed again, freezing her smile in place.

She leaned to Yu-Chen. "I need air."

"I'll go with you."

He started to follow. She stopped him with a hand to his arm. "You're the guest of honor. Stay."

Mrs. Chen intercepted her near the door, balancing a tray piled high. "Almond cookies — prosperity and good fortune!" Her smile was warm, but there was a certain gravity in her eyes. She carefully set her tray down on a nearby table, folding two almond cookies into a red napkin. She pressed the bundle gently into Paige's hand.

"These aren't just for eating. There's a tradition — one for you, one to leave out tonight."

Paige arched a brow. "Leave one out?"

Mrs. Chen's gaze flicked toward the darkening street outside the shop windows. She lowered her voice. "The Hungry Ghost Festival. The spirits roam this month. Not a good night to walk alone, dear."

Paige managed a wry smile, masking a small prick of unease. "I'm a cop."

Mrs. Chen's eyes glimmered with something ancient and knowing. "Cops still have souls. It's important to respect the spirits, especially this month."

"This month?"

A shadow seemed to pass over Mrs. Chen's face. "The Hungry Ghost Festival is a time when the gates between our world and the spirit realm open wide. The spirits of those who have nowhere to rest roam freely, searching for what they've lost." Her voice dropped even lower. "Best not to be out after dark, especially alone."

The crowded shop seemed to grow quieter for a moment, the hum of celebration fading into the background as Paige felt an unexpected shiver trace down her spine. Something about Mrs. Chen's tone made the festival sound less like folklore and more like a warning.

"She doesn't believe in that stuff," Yu-Chen said lightly, but there was a softness beneath his words, as if part of him wished she did. "Besides, she'll learn. We've got the rest of our lives."

"Right," Paige said, forcing a polite smile though her thoughts tangled with unease she couldn't quite name.

Just then, someone called Yu-Chen away for more photos. He brushed a quick kiss on Paige's cheek before disappearing into the crowd.

"You take these," she said softly, "one for you, and one to leave out tonight—for the spirits. It's an old tradition. A little respect goes a long way, especially when dealing with the restless dead."

Paige nodded her thanks and slipped the bundle into her purse, the weight of the ritual settling quietly alongside her badge and gun—tools of the rational world she understood, now accompanied by something far older and more mysterious.

As she turned to leave, Paige left *Love Is the Ultimate Medicine* behind on the table, unaware that she was walking away from a secret more valuable than gold.

Chapter 8

Paige stepped out of the bookshop, the door thudding closed behind her. The night air hit her like a reset button. It was cool, quiet, almost too still for a celebration. Laughter and muffled conversation filtered through the shop's old windows behind her, but she couldn't face it. Not yet.

She took a few steps down the sidewalk, her heels clicking against the cement. The storefronts lining Sutter Street were closed, their glass windows reflecting warm strings of party lights from the bookshop.

Across the road, Mrs. Chen's tea shop sat in stillness, its red paper lanterns glowing above the entrance. A small porcelain plate rested on a bamboo stool just outside the door—five perfect oranges arranged beneath a faded photo of an elderly man in a Mao jacket. A single stick of incense burned low beside it, curling smoke drifting into the warm night.

Paige folded her arms and paced, her stomach knotted. *Her* engagement had become everyone else's celebration. And David. God, why had he come? Though the fall air was still warm, a sudden chill slipped beneath her skin.

"Screw it," she muttered.

She dug out her keys and headed for the car parked half a block down. A quick beep unlocked the doors of her blue Chevy Impala. It was a retired police cruiser she'd picked up at auction for next to nothing. It wasn't flashy, but it was trustworthy. And for Paige, trust was in short supply, particularly when it came to people.

Her boots struck the pavement harder now, echoing in the quiet street. She pulled the door open, ready to slide in and disappear.

"You forgot something," said a voice from the darkness.

She froze. The voice was gentle, familiar.

She turned. "Charlie?"

Old Charlie stepped from the shadows beside the alley. He wasn't panhandling. He wasn't coughing. He just stood there, hands at his sides, his expression peaceful.

Paige shut the car door and walked toward him, cautious. "Charlie, what the hell? Why aren't you at the shelter?"

He didn't move. "Can't leave without taking the book."

"What book?"

His face was half-shadowed under the streetlamp, unreadable. The light cut across him like it couldn't quite land.

"The one Yu-Chen gave you."

Paige blinked. "You too? Jesus Christ, did everyone know about my engagement? Even the local panhandler?"

She paced a few steps, jaw clenched, then turned back to him. "I swear, I'm going to strangle Yu-Chen."

"I'm sorry," she added, softer now. "That came out wrong."

Charlie smiled, just a flicker. "He didn't tell me anything."

She squinted at him, trying to read his face. "Charlie... are you using again? Be honest with me. You said you had a job. If you're high, no one's gonna hire you."

"Oh, I started that job the other day," he said. "Didn't work out."

She rubbed her forehead. "Come on. Get in. I'll take you to the shelter."

"It's too late for that."

"Charlie..."

"You were always kind to me, Paige. Not many people are."

Her brow furrowed. "Okay, you're not making sense. That's it. I'm taking you in before Garcia sees you and runs your name. You'll end up in county, and you don't want that." She marched to the car, yanked open the passenger door. "Get in."

No one moved.

She turned. "Charlie?" She jogged back to the streetlamp. "Charlie?"

Gone.

No footsteps. No echo. No trace. Only a faint breeze, stirring the leaves. The air smelled of incense and burnt matches.

Paige exhaled and ran a hand through her hair. "That man is going to drive me crazy," she muttered.

She got into the car, started the engine, and pulled away from the curb—leaving the empty sidewalk behind.

Paige drove in silence, the road ahead empty but for the yellow beams of her headlights. She turned up the heat, but a chill still clung to her arms. Half a mile from her bungalow, a cat darted into the road—striped, fast, gone in a blink.

She slammed the brakes. Tires shrieked. Heart pounding, she threw the car into park and stepped out.

Wind stirred the trees. A whisper of incense rode the air again—faint, but real. Paige looked around, the street empty. No cat. No Charlie. Just the night pressing in.

She climbed back in, locked the doors, and drove the rest of the way without the radio.

Chapter 9

Paige slept curled beneath a navy-blue quilt, the early morning sun filtering through tall windows and pooling across the soft, woven rug. The room was quiet, still. Her safe place.

A tall leafy plant stood in the corner near the dresser, its broad green leaves catching the morning light. A few sprigs of eucalyptus in a bedside vase gave the room a faint, calming scent.

Her cell phone rang.

She flinched awake, heart jumping. The sound cut through the stillness like an alarm.

Groaning, Paige reached toward the nightstand, knocking into the ceramic lamp with her elbow. She blinked blearily at the screen.

"Seriously? The station? At this hour?"

She swiped to answer. "Helga, this better be—"

She sat up straight. "Chief Jones? ... What? ... Where?"

Her feet hit the floor. She was already moving.

The beams of the 1893 truss bridge loomed overhead, rusted and skeletal against the brightening sky. Below, the river moved slow and cold. Paige pulled up near the gravel turnout, dust kicking up behind her tires.

A squad car was already parked crooked near the path. Crime scene tape fluttered near the tree line.

She spotted Officer White standing near the edge of the trail, arms crossed, watching as a man in a white protective suit knelt beside the body.

Paige slammed her car door and jogged toward them. “Mike, is it...”

White didn’t look at her. “It’s him,” he said quietly. “It’s Charlie. I’m sorry.”

Her stomach sank. She pushed past him.

The man in the hazmat suit stood. He pulled off the hood. It was Yu-Chen.

His face softened the moment he saw her. “Paige. I’m sorry about your friend. I know you tried to help him.”

Her jaw clenched. “Show me.”

Yu-Chen led her to the body. Charlie was covered with a white sheet, still and small beneath it.

Yu-Chen crouched, pulled the sheet back from the arm, and rolled up the sleeve with gloved hands.

Three puncture marks dotted Charlie’s inner elbow—clean, deliberate.

Paige stared. Her breath caught.

“The removal team is prepping to move him now,” said Yu-Chen.

“That fast?”

“We... got here about four hours ago,” Yu-Chen said.

Paige shook her head and stepped back, her grief cracking into fury.

She marched back over to White. “How long have you been here?”

“A couple hours,” he said without flinching.

“Bullshit. Why wasn’t I called in?”

“I passed it on to Helga,” he said. “Maybe she forgot.”

“Right,” she snapped. “So, the chief had to call me directly?”

White shrugged. “Relax. It’s just a dead homeless guy.”

Paige nearly punched him.

Seeing Paige angry, Yu-Chen rushed over. Tried to calm her. "Paige... I should've called you. Mike said he'd take care of it, and I—" he shook his head. "I got caught up with the body. I'm sorry."

She didn't answer. Her eyes stayed fixed on the sheet.

"I should've taken Charlie to the shelter," she said. "Maybe he'd still be alive. This is on me."

They stood in silence as two men in protective suits, the removal team, lifted the body with practiced care, settling it onto the gurney. A moment later, the van doors closed with a soft, final thud.

"I just saw him," she whispered. "After the party. He was right there—talking to me."

Yu-Chen frowned. "Paige... he's been dead at least twenty-four hours. Body temp confirms it."

"No." Her voice cracked. "That's not possible. I saw him."

"You were upset. The proposal. The crowd. Maybe—"

"I *saw* him," she said, louder this time. "He spoke to me. He knew about the book."

Yu-Chen didn't argue. But something in his face changed.

She turned away, breath shallow. Her thoughts spun. She walked off toward the riverbank, trying to ground herself.

Then—*ringing*.

A faint sound. Tinny. Muffled. A phone.

She froze, listened, then moved toward the brush. The sound came again—sharp, buried. She crouched and spotted it under a bush, half-hidden beneath a crushed water bottle and dry leaves.

Charlie's burner phone. The same one he'd flashed two days ago, grinning like it held his ticket out.

"Yu-Chen!" she shouted. "Gloves. Now."

He rushed over, dug into his kit, and handed her a clean pair. She yanked them on and carefully picked up the phone.

Before she could speak, White came charging over. "Paige! Don't touch that!"

She answered but said nothing. The line crackled, then a voice, raspy and cold, came on.

"Charlie? Where the hell are you?"

Paige's pulse quickened. She recognized the accent—a growl more than a cadence—Snake. Hyde's muscle.

She glanced at White: blank face, unreadable. Had he set this up? Was he covering for Snake?

Paige spoke, measured. "He can't answer, Snake."

A beat of silence. Then the line went dead.

Yu-Chen's face drained of color.

"Goddammit, Paige!" White barked, rushing over. "You don't touch evidence—"

"Evidence of *what*, Mike?" she snapped. "A burner phone from a dead man?"

White muttered a curse under his breath. It was too late to cover the slip.

"Bag it, Yu-Chen," he growled.

Yu-Chen took the phone from Paige and slid it into an evidence bag. White snatched it away and stormed off, throwing over his shoulder, "I'll see you at the station."

Once he was out of earshot, Paige turned to Yu-Chen.

"Those needle marks on Charlie's arm," she said, voice low and sharp. "Tell me you and Hyde aren't testing your miracle cure on humans."

Yu-Chen looked away. "No. God, no. He asked—more than once—but I refused. When he pushed again last week, I'd had enough. I filed the paperwork to dissolve the partnership yesterday."

"You did?"

"Yes," he said, panic rising. "But maybe... maybe we're wrong. He wasn't supposed to have access. I kept everything locked down. I ran every trial myself. But what if he tried to replicate it?

Yu-Chen paced.

"God, it was meant to change lives, not take them," Yu-Chen said, his voice cracking. "And now he'll push his own knockoff. He'll tie my name to it, hijack everything I built."

"Yu-Chen," Paige said, stepping in front of him. "Stop. Look at me."

He froze.

She held his gaze. "Hyde has people everywhere. Snake's always lurking at the edge—the kind who gets his hands dirty for cash." She hesitated, remembering how Mike had snapped at her, grabbed evidence, shut down questions. For the first time, Paige questioned if Mike, her cop partner, was involved in this mess.

"Maybe Hyde found out you wanted out. Maybe he recreated your formula or a bastardized version of it. And then used Charlie as a test case."

She looked toward the trees where White had stalked off, his fists clenched and jaw twitching. Something about his mood lately wasn't right.

Her voice slipped low, careful. "We don't know how deep this goes. I don't trust anyone in this. Not Snake, not Hyde, not even White."

Yu-Chen warned, "Hyde could bury us."

She set her jaw, eyes hard as flint. "Let him try."

Yu-Chen swallowed. "What do we do now?"

Paige squared up, glancing down the empty road and back at Yu-Chen. "We dig. We watch every move. We find out who's pulling the strings—Snake, Hyde, whoever's still crawling late at night.

Yu-Chen forced himself to ask, afraid of the answer. "Then what?

She smiled without humor, fire burning in her gut.

"We bury the bastard. One way or another."

Chapter 10

The black Chevy Tahoe rolled to a slow stop at the end of a cracked dirt road, its tires crunching over brittle weeds and scattered gravel. The grass on either side was overgrown, untouched, the kind of place even kids stopped daring each other to explore. No one came out here anymore. And that's exactly why White had. He killed the engine.

Rain threatened overhead, a dull weight pressing down through the low-hanging clouds, but White still wore sunglasses. He didn't care if it looked stupid. He needed to keep his eyes hidden. He was sweating under the old army-green jacket, but it made him feel less like a target.

The warehouse loomed ahead. It was a two-story relic of red brick and busted windows, forgotten by everyone except the rats and whatever scumbag still used it after dark. Concrete walls at the base were stained and scarred, the white metal door in the center streaked with rust. A second-story door hung half off its hinges like a drunken dare to climb.

White stepped out, boots crunching against gravel and broken glass. He adjusted the waistband of his jeans, glancing back down the road. No one. Good.

He didn't want to be here. Hell, he shouldn't be here. But here he was, six foot four of "please-don't-notice-me" in a town where everyone knew his truck, his size, and his reputation. It was almost funny. Almost.

The door creaked open, slow and aching. Hyde stood framed in the gloom. His silver hair was immaculate, suit like it had stepped out of a showroom. And just off his shoulder, leaning casually against the wall, was Snake. Shaved head gleaming under the dim light, dark blazer, arms folded. His eyes tracked every move White made with the same slow, predatory focus White remembered from the motel night.

"You're late," Hyde called, his voice slick and unhurried.

Snake didn't move from his post. He just let his gaze linger on White for a beat longer than necessary before shifting it to the rest of the warehouse, like cataloguing exits.

White removed his sunglasses, forcing himself to ignore Snake's flat stare as he stepped forward. "I don't jump when you whistle."

"Careful," Hyde said as White's boot scraped over a loose piece of metal; it pitched with a hollow groan. "You're standing over the old storeroom. Hatch is rusted through. Wouldn't want you vanishing mid-step. I need your mobile."

White steadied himself. "Look, I've done everything you asked. Museum job, cover stories, clean-up. I'm not your damn delivery boy."

Hyde smiled, eyes cold. "Oh, Michael. One messy motel scene, and you act like I asked for your kidney."

White's jaw tightened. "That guy's not even cold, and Paige is already sniffing around. Why'd you drag that homeless guy into this?"

Hyde shrugged. "I needed his data. Yu-Chen's formula changed everything. But a cure like that doesn't come from luck. It comes from precision. Ratios. Chemistry."

White scoffed. "You said it was the gold dust. Said it had to be old. So, I hit the museum like you wanted. No gold dust in those old jeans after all."

Hyde's grin thinned. "At first, I believed him. He said he found gold dust trapped in amber, buried after that hundred-year flood. Plausible enough. But now I see it for what it was—misdirection. The real breakthrough wasn't the gold itself. It was what he did to it."

White's gaze dropped. "So all this... was for nothing?"

"No. Process of elimination. We're chasing a miracle. This isn't just medicine. It's billions."

White muttered, "And you really think you'll crack Yu-Chen's formula without him?"

"I don't need to be a genius," Hyde said. "Just access — his notes, his lab. Once I isolate the variables, I'll replicate and improve it."

White shifted, feeling Snake's unblinking eyes on him again from near the door.

Hyde smiled, cruel and quiet. "A few fresh trials are all I need."

White flinched. "You mean warm bodies."

Hyde spread his hands. "You call them that. I call them opportunity."

"This is it," White said. "No more favors. If Paige finds out—"

Hyde's tone hardened. "You'll lose your badge. Your pension. Your freedom. And let's not forget that motel mess."

White didn't answer. Snake pushed off the wall, crossing just close enough to brush White's shoulder on his way to open the warehouse door. He didn't say a word, but the smirk that ghosted his mouth said plenty.

Hyde straightened his tie. "We're almost there, Mike. Don't screw it up."

The warehouse door slammed shut behind them with a sharp metallic clang, the sound rattling through the space like a warning.

White's gaze drifted to the rusted hatch in the center of the floor, half-buried under a torn sheet of plywood. The metal was pitted and flaking, the edges eaten away like rot in bone. A faint draft seeped up through the cracks, cold against his ankles.

He stepped back without meaning to.

Some places you just knew not to stand too long.

The sky above the warehouse was a blank, tarnished blue, the crumbling brick walls casting long shadows on the weed-choked gravel. Hyde stepped out into the sunlight, trailing cigarette smoke as Snake detached himself from the doorway and fell into step beside him.

Snake's gaze flicked over the battered Chevy Tahoe parked crooked in the lot.

"White's losing his edge," Snake muttered, voice low but perfectly audible. "Worried about the cops, second-guessing every move. Guys like that crack when things go sideways."

Hyde didn't respond right away, eyes scanning the ruined windows and warped doors. The wind rustled through the high grass, carrying the faint tang of rust and rain. Snake tucked his hands behind his back, waiting—coiled, like he was about to pounce.

"Stealing lab notes isn't complicated," Snake continued. "If it needs doing right, I'll do it. No drama. No mess."

Hyde lit a cigarette, taking his time. "You volunteering?"

Snake snorted, jerking his head back toward the warehouse.

"I'm saying, if those lab notes are the real deal, that's not chump change we're talking about. That's a fat, ugly fortune. Billion-with-a-B kind of money. Whoever puts that in your hand? They're set for life. Houses, cars, women... the works."

Hyde's smile curled thin through a stream of smoke. "And you figure you could earn yourself a seat at that table?"

Snake smirked, "You'll get what you want. I always deliver."

Hyde studied him a beat longer, the cigarette ember flaring. "I can always count on you to do the math, Snake. Most men just see a job. You? You already see the endgame."

Snake didn't answer, but the corner of his mouth twitched. It was the closest he got to a smile.

Hyde flicked ash onto the cracked concrete, turning for his car. "Stay close. This could get interesting."

As the Porsche's engine growled to life, Snake stayed on the cracked pavement, eyes on the empty road. Calculating. Waiting. In his head, the job was already his. It was just a matter of letting White fail first.

Chapter 11

Yu-Chen stepped out of Black Core Labs and into the crisp afternoon light. He hadn't meant to walk this far, but the weight of Hyde's threats pushed him forward, fast. He hadn't even realized he was still wearing his lab coat.

And then he spotted her.

Paige.

Out for her afternoon run. Right, it was her day off. He still wasn't used to seeing her out here—off duty, relaxed. Earbuds in. Unbothered. Calm before the storm.

"Paige!" he shouted.

She slowed, tugging out one earbud as she turned.

"Yu-Chen?"

He jogged toward her, lab coat flapping.

"What are you doing out here?" she asked, startled. "You look—what's going on?"

"We need to talk," he said, taking her arm and guiding her off the main path.

They stopped beneath a line of trees, near a quiet bench.

"Let's sit."

Paige looked at him, concerned, then nodded. They sat.

"I ended my partnership with Hyde," Yu-Chen said.

Her eyes searched his.

"Because of Charlie?"

"Yes. And because Hyde's escalating. He's threatened to shut down my work. He's dangerous. If I push too hard now—if I call for an autopsy—I could lose the lab, the funding, everything. But if Charlie was dosed with the compound... it could tie Hyde to human trials."

Paige stood, pacing.

"I told you he'd try to cut you out. Now people are dying. I need to get a warrant for Black Core. Judge Clark will back me."

"Paige, listen, please. I'm close. I'm running final-phase viability testing. One more protocol, and I can prove the compound stabilizes in mammalian tissue. This isn't just about plants anymore. We're talking about real applications, life-saving applications."

"Charlie's dead, Yu-Chen. Or is he just another data point to you?"

"No, it's not that. It's the bigger picture. If I lose access to the lab now, the data's gone. Everything's gone. Just give me forty-eight hours. Please."

"You want me to sit on this? Let Hyde keep testing on people?"

"I'm not defending him. But if I don't finish this now, I may never get another chance. Paige, this cure could save thousands of lives."

"You're giving him room to kill again."

"We don't know Charlie died from the compound—"

"Seriously?" she snapped. "You're backing off now?"

"That came out wrong. I just meant—let's wait for the results."

"Charlie's dead. You said yourself, Hyde was using human subjects. What happens when the next body drops?"

Yu-Chen swallowed, trying to stay calm.

"Monday morning. Under the bridge. You said you saw Charlie—right before they took him."

"Yeah. So?"

"I got the preliminary report. He'd been dead almost forty-eight hours. Paige... you couldn't have seen him."

A beat.

"You think I imagined him?"

"No. I think... I believe you. You saw something. Do you know what the Hungry Ghost Festival is?"

"I don't have time for this."

She stood. He followed.

"Just hear me out. In Chinese tradition, ghosts of those who die under wrongful circumstances walk among the living this month. Maybe what you saw wasn't Charlie... but what's left when justice hasn't been served."

"Great. So now I'm supposed to drop a murder case because of superstition?"

"Not drop it. Just... delay. Please, leave town. Tonight. Just for a few days. Let me finish this. Let me protect you."

"I can't walk away from my job."

"I'll handle Hyde. Once the last protocol is done, I'll go public. We'll be free. I just need time."

Paige stood still, eyes locked on Yu-Chen.

"So your career comes first."

Yu-Chen shook his head, voice low. "No, Paige, I want a life with you. But I can't get free of Hyde overnight. I have to end this the right way."

"You want to build a future with me by letting a killer walk?"

"I'm not letting him walk. I'm finishing what I started. Then I expose him. With evidence. Not guesswork."

She stepped back, arms crossed. "Charlie's in the morgue. Hyde's out there making calls to a dead man's phone. And you're still in your lab coat talking about vision and timing."

"Please, just leave town. Give me time. Do it for us."

Her voice cracked, sharp, restrained.

"If 'us' means standing by while Hyde keeps testing on people, I want no part of it."

She turned.

"Paige, wait. Just wait."

She stopped.

"I can request the autopsy," he said. "If Charlie's body shows any trace of the compound—especially gold particulate—it could tie Hyde to the failed replication. That would be enough to go after him."

Paige turned, hope flickering in her eyes. "Then do it. Yu-Chen, that could be the break we need. I know it risks your funding, but that's replaceable. This—Charlie—isn't."

Yu-Chen hesitated. He could already feel the fallout—Hyde freezing the lab, pulling the plug, burying everything. He swallowed.

"Just... wait a few more days. A week at most. I'm so close, Paige. One more round of trials. I swear I'm almost there."

Her face hardened.

"So your gold dust comes before justice?"

"No. I mean, yes. I mean..." He faltered. "I just need more time."

"You'll always need more time. You'll always have another excuse, another breakthrough that's more important than..." She stopped herself.

"Than what?"

She met his eyes, something raw and uncertain there. "Than us. Than figuring out if we even work."

"What are you saying?"

“I don't know, Yu-Chen. I honestly don't know.”

She turned and walked away.

Yu-Chen didn’t move. Breath shallow. Hands clenched.

“That came out all wrong,” he whispered.

But she was already gone.

Chapter 12

The overhead lights hummed, steady and cold, blending with the whir of centrifuges and fans. Rows of flasks shimmered gold on the cluttered workbench, casting slow, wavering shadows

Yu-Chen slumped in the chair, shoulders heavy, the weight of another life-altering choice pressing down.

Then, he straightened.

He couldn't stall any more. Not with Charlie dead. Not with Paige watching. He set his jaw and began to type—fast, deliberate, as if slowing down might make him stop.

The town's autopsy database wasn't meant to be accessed from Hyde's lab, but he'd rerouted the network, bypassed the firewall. A few keystrokes now, and everything could unravel.

He typed only a few sentences, but words that would change his life. He stared at the screen.

Request: Full autopsy on Charles Ng. Authorization: Dr. Huang Yu-Chen, Consulting Forensic Pathologist, Folsom Police Department. Toxicology screening requested: Full metabolic panel, foreign compounds, and trace metal analysis.

His finger hovered over *Send*.

He imagined the fallout. Hyde discovering the request. Pulling the funding. Freezing the lab. Seizing the gold dust. Dismantling everything.

And yet, Charlie was dead. And Paige was right.

Yu-Chen closed his eyes. Exhaled. Pressed *Send*.

The confirmation blinked on screen. There was no undoing it now.

He leaned back in the chair, the silence collapsing in around him like a vacuum.

"That's the nail in the coffin, Doctor Hyde," he murmured.

Behind him, a click. Footsteps.

"And what nail would that be?" came the low, even voice.

Yu-Chen stood up too fast. "How did you—? The door was locked."

Hyde stepped inside like he owned the place. Because, in a way, he did. Unreadable, calm, perfectly put-together.

A second figure followed him in. He was tall, broad-shouldered, his head shaved to a shine that caught the fluorescents. Yu-Chen didn't need an introduction to know this was not a man who came along for conversation.

"You forget, Yu-Chen," Hyde said, "I hold the master key."

The stranger, Snake, shut the door behind them and took up position there, silent and still, a barrier as absolute as a locked vault.

Hyde's eyes flicked over the lab, lingering on the microscope, the notebooks, the flasks of burnt gold solution.

"I think we ended yesterday's conversation on a sour note. I wanted you to know you have my utmost support and financial backing."

Yu-Chen kept his eyes on the man by the door.

Hyde followed his gaze. "Relax. Just security. I've had concerns about break-ins recently. Snake won't be needed tonight."

He motioned lightly. Snake gave a single nod and slipped out the door, silent as a ghost.

The door whispered shut behind him. Silence returned, but it wasn't peace. It was pressure, tightening around the room like a noose.

This wasn't a conversation. It was a test. Hyde was probing, watching for any hint that Yu-Chen knew—about Paige, about Charlie's phone, about the ghost of a man whose body would soon confirm everything.

"There's a path forward," Hyde said, almost soothing. "You need funding. I need vision. We revise the contract, scale the application. Not just dead plants, but for real recovery. Human trials. And I already have access to willing participants."

Yu-Chen met his eyes. "Willing? Or just desperate homeless men?

Hyde's smile twisted.

"Charlie wasn't the first homeless man to die recently. And you keep talking about having access to 'willing participants.' Snake's been busy, hasn't he?"

Hyde's expression didn't change. "Correlation isn't causation, Yu-Chen. You're a scientist. You know better than to leap to conclusions."

"You're already testing a bootleg version of my compound," Yu-Chen cut in. "You're trying to clone it. But you don't have the right precursors, the stabilizer blend. None of it. And you never will. I won't let you sabotage this cure before it has a chance to change lives."

Hyde straightened, tone colder. "Feed the world, yes—but why stop there? We could cure major diseases like cancer and Alzheimer's. You found a shiny ingredient, Yu-Chen. That doesn't make you indispensable. You were a scientist-for-hire. This cure will happen, with or without you."

Hyde stepped closer. "I want a sample. By tomorrow."

Yu-Chen didn't blink. "You've already tried. Without my consent. And someone died. I warned you. I have no choice but to dissolve the partnership."

Hyde's voice cooled. "You always have a choice, Yu-Chen."

"And since I own your debt, your lab, and your pipeline, I have every right to take control."

He smiled, coldly.

"Oh, and do give my regards to your fiancée. Word is she's in line for chief of police. Would be tragic if politics got in the way."

The door clicked shut behind him.

Yu-Chen slammed his palm across the bench. Pages scattered. Breath tight, he gripped the edge of the table, eyes locked on the drawer.

Now he understood the truth.

Hyde wouldn't stop. Not ever.

Chapter 13

Paige's pulse still hammered from the fight with Yu-Chen. Sweat clung to her collarbone, her breaths sharp and shallow as she pounded down the trail. She replayed his words with every step. He accused her of not understanding, of rushing into danger. Maybe he was right. Maybe they were both too stubborn to make this work.

She hadn't even made it a quarter mile when she saw him.

David.

Standing near the water's edge, hands in his pockets, staring at the lake like it might speak first. A place they used to walk at sunset, back when everything had felt simple.

She turned too late.

"Paige?"

She winced and stopped, her heart already racing for reasons that had nothing to do with running. He was already walking toward her, that familiar careful stride she'd once found comforting.

"Nice day for a run," he offered, his voice carrying that same gentle uncertainty it always had around her.

"Yeah." The word came out breathier than she'd intended.

A pause stretched between them, filled with the sound of water lapping against the shore and distant traffic. The same sounds that used to be the soundtrack to their evening walks.

"Sorry for crashing the engagement thing."

"That what people are calling it?" She gave a short laugh, wiping sweat from her forehead. "Felt more like an ambush."

"Still. I shouldn't have come." His eyes searched her face, looking for something she wasn't sure she wanted him to find.

She shrugged, trying for casual. "It's over."

They looked at each other across the small space that felt like an ocean. So many things to say, but she couldn't think of one that wouldn't change everything.

"You two setting a date?"

Her jaw tightened. A noose, that's what it felt like—the question, the expectation, the future everyone seemed to want for her more than she wanted it herself. She didn't answer right away, her gaze drifting to the water where a pair of ducks moved in perfect synchronization.

"Too soon to say."

David nodded, glanced at the ground, then back at her. When he spoke again, his voice was quieter, more serious.

"I wanted you to hear it from me. I'm joining Doctors Without Borders."

Her breath caught, and she felt something shift in her chest. Was it surprise, panic, loss? What?

"I've been thinking about it for a while now. They've fast-tracked my application." He was watching her reaction carefully, as if her response might change his mind.

She studied him, noting the way he stood straighter when he talked about it, the spark in his eyes she hadn't seen in months. "Since when?"

"Couple of days."

The timing hit her like a cold wave. A couple of days, right around when Yu-Chen had proposed. They both knew what that meant, the elephant standing right there between them on the jogging path.

He forced a smile that didn't quite reach his eyes. "New chapter. I always said I wanted to travel. Figured now's the time."

The words stung more than they should have. She was engaged to another man, after all. She had no right to feel abandoned.

"You mean now that we're not..." she stopped herself, the words too dangerous to finish. "You mean now that it's convenient."

"I leave in two days." The finality in his voice made her stomach drop. "I've got twenty-four hours to change my mind."

She folded her arms across her chest, partly from the cooling sweat, partly as armor. "Why would you?"

The question came out sharper than she'd intended, but something in David's expression shifted. It could have been hope or recognition. They stood in the silence, the question hanging heavier than either expected, while the lake continued its gentle rhythm beside them.

"Because I need to know if there's still something here," he said. "Between us."

Her eyes searched his. "You're asking me that *now*?"

"I saw your face when Yu-Chen proposed. You care about him. But you didn't look in love."

"So, you want me to dump him right now? Clock's ticking, right? Give you a reason to stay?"

"I'm saying I'll walk away from the whole thing. If you tell me there's still something here."

"You should've said that a long time ago," Paige said, her voice steady but brittle. "When it would've mattered."

She stepped back, the old hurt rising to the surface.

"I don't disappear when things get hard. But you do. You always find something more important than us when it gets real. A job, a program, an opportunity you can't miss.' And I'm tired of being the thing you walk away from."

He didn't respond. Didn't need to.

"Run off to whatever country makes you feel better about leaving."

She turned and ran, breath sharp, chest tighter than it had been all morning.

David stood there, watched her go. He didn't answer. He just turned, his gaze drifting back to the water. Like it might finally tell him what he should've said, back when he still had time.

Chapter 14

The fluorescents hummed overhead, cold and steady. In the stillness of the lab, Yu-Chen stood at his workbench, shoulders tight, carefully guiding the last of the gold dust into two sachets no bigger than teabags. One lot had already been smuggled out, hidden in the book he gave Paige when he proposed. Now only these two remained. And he was determined that Hyde would never touch them.

A sharp knock echoed from the lab door.

Yu-Chen looked up. Through the narrow glass panel, he saw the familiar silhouette, shoulders squared, satchel slung across one arm.

Mr. Yeung.

Yu-Chen buzzed him in.

The lock clicked open. Mr. Yeung stepped inside with quiet purpose. His tone, as always, carried a trace of dry wit.

"I brought what you asked," he said. "You said it was urgent."

He lifted the satchel.

"Was anyone at the gate?" Yu-Chen asked.

"Night guard checked my bag. Probably wondered why I've got a book on Taoist alchemy at this hour. I found it right where you said, beneath the third floorboard left of your dresser. Strange hiding spot for bedtime reading."

He handed over the hardcover. *The Elixir of Life – The Origin of Taoist Alchemy.*

Yu-Chen gave a faint smile but said nothing. He wanted to explain, to tell him everything—but even a hint might allow the wrong people to connect the dots.

"It was safer that way," he said.

He turned to the bench and retrieved a utility blade from the drawer. With steady hands, he sliced into the book's inner spine, peeling it open to reveal the hollowed-out channel he'd carved days earlier. He picked up one of the sachets—its contents shimmered under the fluorescents, a ripple of gold in the sterile light.

Mr. Yeung watched.

"Is that the gold dust? The secret ingredient to your miracle cure?"

Yu-Chen nodded. "Yes. I want you to give this book to my father. He'll keep it safe."

"You already gave one lot to Paige, hidden in that book with the engagement ring," Mr. Yeung said. "Now another to your father. Smart to split them up. If Hyde discovers one stash..."

Yu-Chen sealed the spine and pressed the edge smooth with his thumb.

"I'm moving the gold dust out of his reach, before he decides it all belongs to him."

Mr. Yeung paused, his gaze shifting to the last sachet on the table. "And the third lot?"

Yu-Chen opened a drawer and retrieved a cloth-wrapped bundle. Inside was a vintage pocket watch. Its brass casing was tarnished. The Roman numerals were still clear beneath the worn glass, black metal indices untouched by time. Yu-Chen got the pocket watch along with the gold dust from the dead Chinese miner's knapsack. His mentor had discovered the watch was over two centuries old, possibly a gift from a British diplomat to the emperor himself. Something in its history made Yu-Chen feel it was a fitting place to hide the last of the gold dust.

He set the sachet beside it.

"It's the last one. If anything happens to me, I want you to melt it down and coat the watch with the gold. Just a thin layer, enough to leave a trace but not draw attention."

Mr. Yeung's brow creased. "Are you in trouble, Yu-Chen?"

"There's no time to explain. Just promise me you'll do as I ask."

Mr. Yeung glanced at the old pocket watch, hesitation flickering in his eyes. "I understand. But this watch is old. Could fall apart in the process."

"Promise me, Mr. Yeung."

He nodded. "I promise. But let me say this. Paige has only been in your life a few months. You're entrusting her with two out of the three lots of your gold dust. Why her?"

Yu-Chen hesitated, then said, "She's a cop who doesn't flinch in a fight. She stands up to men twice her size, and she believes in justice even when it costs her. But more than that, she's the only person I trust completely. Hyde can't buy her, can't intimidate her, can't manipulate her the way he does everyone else. If something happens to me, she'll know what to do with it."

Mr. Yeung said nothing. He folded the same battered pocket watch Yu-Chen had found in the miner's knapsack back into the cloth, tucked it into the satchel, and fastened it shut.

"Then I'll make sure it goes where it needs to."

They locked eyes for a moment. Nothing more needed to be said.

The hum of the lab returned, clinical and still, as the last of the gold dust disappeared from the bench.

Yu-Chen extended his hand, but Mr. Yeung paused. Instead, he pulled him into a quick, firm hug—uncharacteristic, deeply human.

"You'd better go," Yu-Chen said.

He buzzed the lock. Mr. Yeung stepped out without a word.

Only once the door clicked shut did Yu-Chen turn away, wiping a tear before it could fall.

Chapter 15

The park was deserted. The wind rustled through dry leaves. A single streetlamp buzzed overhead, casting a weak pool of light near the empty benches. Mike White leaned against a picnic table, hoodie up, hands buried in his jacket pockets.

Footsteps approached. Slow. Unhurried.

Doctor Hyde emerged from the shadows, his tailored coat hardly shifting as he moved. He stopped just short of the light, eyes glinting in the dark.

"You trying to blow my cover, Hyde?" White muttered. "This is exactly how that happens."

Hyde didn't smile. He held up his phone. "He ordered an autopsy."

White blew out a breath. "So?"

"If the panel finds gold dust in Charlie's system, we're both exposed. I didn't want him dead. This was supposed to be a controlled trial. But now it's a body on a slab."

White exhaled, sharp and bitter. His jaw tightened as the image returned. He flashed back to the woman in the motel, lips split, bruises darkening around her throat. Said she wanted it rough. Said she could handle it. Then she didn't get back up. Those marks matched his hands—too big, too strong. And Hyde had arranged the scene to read like a textbook overdose. No questions asked. Maybe this autopsy was his shot at freedom. Let Yu-Chen dig. Let Hyde take the fall. And the girl? That wasn't on him. Not really. She made the rules. He just played by them.

He squared his shoulders, the weight shifting. Just a little. But enough.

"I told you this was a bad idea. I didn't sign up to be implicated in your back-alley trials."

Hyde's voice went cold. "My trials? Your snitch was the one who brought in the volunteers. You're implicated, Mike, whether you admit it or not."

White shrugged. "Yu-Chen's not some rookie intern. He's the town's de facto medical examiner. He's got a reason to dig."

Hyde stepped closer. His tone dropped to a hiss. "Then make sure the report never surfaces. Talk to your people at the county. Say it never came through. A network failure. Misfiled paperwork. Whatever you need to say, say it."

"No."

Hyde's brow twitched. "Excuse me?"

"I said no." White's jaw clenched. "I broke into a museum. Killed the cameras. Nabbed those worthless miner jeans. There was no gold dust, no nothing. I'm done."

"You did half a job. And now you're going to finish it."

"I'm not your damn janitor."

Hyde paused. Then, too calm: "If you're worried about exposure, don't be. You're already compromised. Do this right, and no one needs to know."

White stepped back, shaking his head. "You don't get it. I'm not afraid of getting caught. I'm afraid of the day I stop feeling sick about what we do."

He turned to leave.

"You walk away now," Hyde said, "and I'll take everything you've done and turn it over to the press myself. Buried evidence. Museum theft. Evidence tampering. Oh, and let's not forget the woman at the motel. The one I cleaned up after. You want the press changing that overdose to murder?"

White froze. "That was a mistake. A night that got out of hand."

"Don't forget who protected you," Hyde added. "I own your silence. And your future."

White didn't turn around. "You don't own anything but bad timing. Yu-Chen had the guts to finally call you out. Maybe it's my turn to finish what he started and be the one to put cuffs on you."

White disappeared into the dark.

Hyde stood motionless.

He looked down at his phone.

And did nothing.

His jaw tightened. One gloved hand curled into a fist. For the first time in years, he had no backup plan, no loyal errand boy to mop up the mess. Just the wind, the dark, and a body in the morgue that threatened to unravel everything.

He turned toward the shadows, lips pressed into a hard line.

This wasn't over.

Chapter 16

Paige's shoes pounded the trail, breath ragged as the path blurred past. She hadn't planned to run this far. But her legs kept moving, as if distance could quiet the churn in her chest. David's words echoed louder with every step.

"I'm saying I'll walk away from the whole thing. If you tell me there's still something here."

She wasn't sure what hit harder—his question, or the chance she'd just thrown away to answer it honestly.

Yu-Chen was a good man. But she couldn't lie to him. Not about this. Not anymore.

She rounded the last bend and saw his cottage ahead. Her pace slowed, resolve tightening like a knot in her ribs. It was time.

Soft light spilled through the front windows of Yu-Chen's cottage, catching on the edge of the desk where he sat in jeans and a T-shirt, bare feet resting on warm floorboards. The room was still, save for the occasional creak of the wood-paneled ceiling above him and the scratch of pen on paper.

He read the words aloud as he wrote, his voice a whisper.

"Paige, I'm sorry we fought. I should've told you sooner. I'm proud of you. I've always been proud of you. One day, you'll probably be Chief. You asked me to do the right thing, and I did. I requested the autopsy, just like you said. I risked it all—my research, my future—because doing what's right mattered more. Because you matter more. Love, Yu-Chen."

He set the pen down, staring at the card for a long moment, heart pounding harder than it should've.

A knock shattered the quiet.

He glanced at the clock. It was barely 6 a.m. He padded barefoot across the cottage to the black-framed door. Through the glass, Paige stood outside, flushed from her run, arms folded tight, her expression stormy.

He looked down, her card still clutched in his hand. Wordlessly, he set it on the console table by the door, the ink on the envelope still fresh. Then he opened the door. "Paige?' he said, surprised. 'What are you doing here?"

She pushed past him into the entryway, voice tight. "I need to tell you something. I couldn't wait."

He shut the door behind her, startled. "I was just about to—"

"I need to say this first," she interrupted, her words tumbling out fast. "Yu-Chen, I can't marry you. I'm sorry."

His breath caught. The corners of his vision seemed to blur. "Wait—what? Is this about Hyde? If you're worried—"

"It's not Hyde." Her voice broke. "It's me. We rushed into this. We've only been together a few months."

"But you're the one, Paige." His voice cracked despite himself, rawer than he intended. "I love you. I want a life with you."

She looked like she might cry, but didn't.

It hit him in waves—the memory of her 'yes,' the relief he'd clung to, the fragile picture of a future built around her. He remembered how he had rehearsed that proposal, fingers numbed with sweat, believing he had found something unshakable. Now he watched her shoulders curl inward, as if she were folding herself away from him.

For a fleeting second, denial fought to take hold. Maybe she was scared. Maybe she needed reassurance, space, patience. Those things he could give her. Things he wanted to give. But beneath her words, there was something final in her eyes, like a locked door he would never step through.

"You're a good man, Yu-Chen. But I've made my decision. I'm sorry."

Before he could gather breath, his phone buzzed on the hallway table. The sound was jarring, cruelly ordinary. He glanced at the screen.

County Morgue.

His stomach tightened. He grabbed it. "Dr. Murphy... yeah, I submitted the request... now's not—" He covered the receiver with his hand, helpless anger trembling through him. "Paige, just give me a second—"

"I can't." Her voice was barely audible.

He turned toward the kitchen, forcing his voice low into the phone. "Just give me five minutes. I'll call you back."

When he came back to the living room, she was gone.

Her engagement ring sat on the console table, catching the pale morning light. It rested atop his card. The one where he had written, in his careful hand, that he'd risked everything for her.

Silence pressed in from every corner of the house. He could still feel her presence in the air, like a door left open letting in the cold, but she was already gone. And all at once, the stillness felt permanent.

Chapter 17

Old Town Folsom stirred to life under the warm afternoon sun. Golden light spilled across the crooked brick facades and slanted rooftops of Sutter Street. The scent of espresso drifted from the matte-blue coffee truck idling near the Gaslight Building, mingling with the faint hum of traffic and shopfront chatter.

Officer Mike White stood at the window, hands shoved in his jacket pockets, waiting for his coffee. His eyes were still red from the night before. He hadn't slept. Couldn't. Not with Charlie in the morgue and Yu-Chen breathing down everyone's neck.

"Good afternoon, Officer."

The voice came from behind him—smooth, pleasant, and dangerous.

White turned. "Hyde. You lost, or just feeling bold?"

Doctor Hyde stepped into the light, holding a manila envelope like it weighed nothing. Dressed in a tailored linen blazer and crisp slacks, he looked more like a politician than a biotech tycoon. There was no warmth behind the smile. Only calculation.

"No need to be rude. I was just headed over to the Folsom Chronicle. Thought I'd drop something off." He gave the envelope a casual pat. "Enjoy your coffee."

White's jaw worked, eyes narrowing. He was about to snap when he noticed movement across the street.

Snake leaned against his parked motorcycle, sunglasses on, cigarette burning down between his fingers. Not watching Hyde exactly, not watching White either. He was just… there. But that was the problem. Snake's stillness felt sharper than anyone else's motion. Like the whole street had been arranged for his convenience.

White looked away fast, throat dry.

He cursed under his breath, tossed his cup in the trash, and caught up to Hyde fast.

"Hey, what the hell are you doing?"

Hyde didn't break stride. "Just exercising my civic duty. Whistleblower protections are very trendy these days."

White grabbed his arm and yanked him into the shadowed doorway of a closed hat shop, its hand-painted Back After Lunch sign hanging crooked in the window.

"You said we were square. I did everything you asked."

Hyde lifted the envelope between two fingers, casual as a magician about to reveal a trick.

"And yet here I am with a folder full of screenshots from the motel's CCTV. Your rental car caught in the frame, timestamp and all. That kind of evidence tends to change a man's priorities."

White blinked. "Footage? That was a year ago. They wipe the drives every week."

Hyde's smile spread slowly, indulgent. "Ordinarily, yes. But Snake paid the clerk a visit the very next morning. The man left suddenly, and his replacement proved much more… cooperative. The footage migrated to a safer vault. It's amazing what a few underpaid employees will overlook, for the right price."

He tilted his head, savoring White's panic. "And then there's the call you made to me that night. It's in my records, Officer. The one where you begged me to clean up your mess."

White's jaw tightened. "It was an accident. She... she wanted it rough."

Hyde's smile was all ice. "And the SFPD just chalked her up to another overdose. Lucky you. But imagine if the Chronicle ran the full story, with pictures. What would that do for your reputation?"

They stood for a long beat. White's pulse thudded in his temples. He risked a glance out onto the street

Snake was still there, leaning against his motorcycle, smoke curling from his hand. Watching now. Waiting.

White swallowed. "What do you want?"

Hyde's voice dropped, silky and precise. "Yu-Chen's research. Notes. His test compound. The gold dust. There were three lots. He's likely hidden them, but you've got the tools to find them."

White stared. "You want me to steal from his lab?"

Hyde's eyes glittered. "Steal... clean up... call it what you like. One less competitor makes for quieter waters."

The meaning landed, heavy and sharp. White's face drained of color.

His jaw tightened. "No. I'm not doing that."

White's voice cracked as he shoved the manila envelope hard against Hyde's chest. The sharp edge creased Hyde's suit for an instant.

"Find another errand boy."

Hyde's smile didn't falter. "Suit yourself."

White stormed off down Sutter Street, shoving past a pair of tourists, his shoulders rigid with rage.

From across the street, Snake moved. He crushed the last ember of his cigarette beneath his boot and crossed to Hyde without hurry, quiet as a shadow.

Hyde glanced at him, the picture of satisfaction. “Our friend is squeamish.”

Snake didn’t answer. He just looked down the block where White had gone, then back to Hyde. His silence said enough.

Hyde moved to a sidewalk trash bin, opened the envelope, and pulled out a stack of blank printer paper. As he let it fall, the edge of the envelope caught his wrist. One of his sapphire cufflinks slipped free, hit the concrete, and rolled beneath the bin, hidden in the shadows.

Hyde fastened his jacket—a single sapphire glinted from his right cuff, the left now bare. He never looked down.

“We’ll handle it another way,” he said softly.

Snake gave the faintest nod, as if receiving orders without words.

After Hyde left, Snake strolled over to the trash bin. Kneeling, he picked up the lost cufflink—a flash of blue in the dusty light. He tucked it in his pocket before melting away down the street.

Chapter 18

The bullpen sat in a dull hush, lit by a grid of flickering fluorescents. Four desks formed a square outside the chief's glass-walled office, blinds drawn tight. The scent of burnt coffee lingered from the morning pot. Somewhere, a printer jammed and groaned without resolve.

Paige sat stiff at her desk, her patrol jacket draped over the back of her chair. The screen in front of her showed the museum break-in report. She wasn't reading it. Her fingers hovered on the keyboard, unmoving.

She blinked hard. Wiped the corner of one eye with her knuckle. The movement was quick, practiced, forgotten by the time it landed.

Across from her sat Officer Jamal Jackson, the youngest cop on the force. He was quiet, sharp-eyed, and calmer than most rookies. He leaned back in his chair, a file folder resting in his lap. He watched her a moment, then spoke without looking up.

"You've been staring at that report like it owes you money."

Paige shifted in her seat. "Just checking for follow-ups. Garcia might've missed something."

"I can call him if you want."

She shook her head. "No."

He closed the folder.

"You alright?"

She kept her eyes on the monitor. "Just tired."

He didn't press. "If you want out for a bit, take it. I'll hang around. Paperwork's not going anywhere."

She nudged her chair back. "Think I'll take you up on that."

Jamal slid past with a stack of reports, heading to the break room for fresh coffee.

The phone rang three times, shrill in the quiet. Jamal, buried in the fridge, called out, "You'd better let it ring, Paige. I see you hovering."

The phone kept ringing. Paige lingered, her hand fixed midair. If she left now, the call would vanish into voicemail. Another thing pushed aside. She snatched the receiver.

"Folsom PD, Officer Gold."

A pause. Then a voice: steady, clipped. "Officer Gold, this is Detective Gary Callahan, SFPD. Sorry for the cold call, but I'm hoping you might help me chase a thread. You got a minute?"

She glanced toward the break room. Jamal faced the coffee machine, cursing under his breath.

"Go ahead," she said, shifting her weight.

"We found a body last night. Tony Manelli. Armed robbery, parolee, used to run with Destiny Brown. She died in a motel here about a year ago—overdose, or so it looked. She had a bracelet on her, stolen in an armored car heist. Manelli was in that crew. Most of the loot is still missing, but this bracelet's the only piece we've recovered. The main sapphire is gone."

Paige's pen hovered over her pad. "Neither name rings a bell."

"Didn't expect them to. But the only Folsom link is a rental car. Motel records flagged a plate from your area, the night Destiny died. Renter gave a fake name, but the agency checked out. If you've heard about loose sapphires or anyone suddenly flashing big money, let us know. Anything helps track these jewels."

Paige wrote it down. "Can you send a photo of the bracelet?"

"It's coming through now. Five sapphires in a gold chain, center setting empty. If you hear about anyone selling stones, even months old, give us a nudge."

Her computer chimed. A photo filled the screen: yellow gold, five settings, the largest stone missing.

She asked, "Why not get the driver's ID from the rental place?

Callahan sighed. "The agency changed hands a couple of months after the incident. The chain lost the old records—nothing to pull. Just hoping to shake something loose, maybe someone remembers."

"No rumors about sapphires, but I'll keep my ears open. If something crops up, I'll call."

Callahan replied, "Appreciate the help. We're combing records on our end, but that rental car's still a loose thread.

Paige clicked "Reply," typed her number into the message field, and hit send. "I just emailed you my cell," she said. "Call or text if you find anything on that rental."

"Will do."

Paige set the phone down. Jamal poked his head out of the break room, coffee in hand. "Thought you needed air."

She stared at her screen, where SFO PD's email glowed—the detective's notes, details about the rental car inquiry, and the case from last year. "I do," she said.

Jamal lifted his mug in a lazy salute. "Then go. I've got it here, a fortress of bad coffee and worse paperwork."

He didn't ask about the call or the email on her screen. Paige could feel the questions behind his eyes, but he let them sit, unspoken.

"I thought the chief had you on a ride-along tonight."

"Not till later. Go. You look like you need a break."

Paige hesitated, then nodded. "I just need to walk. That trail by the lake... it helps me breathe."

Paige grabbed her jacket and headed for the back exit. She didn't look back. The doors swung shut behind her with a soft clack that sounded louder than it should've.

This job was supposed to steady her. Give her purpose. But today all it did was remind her that she couldn't keep her personal life separate, no matter how hard she tried. She clenched her jaw and walked faster. Being a cop was the one thing she still wanted more than anything. She just had to hold it together long enough not to lose it.

Jamal watched the door a moment. He sat at his desk and typed on his computer. He pulled up the gold rush museum file Paige had been working on.

He skimmed the log and frowned.

White had already signed off on it. Two hours before Paige had even opened the case.

Weird. Maybe a clerical mix-up.

Jamal leaned back, thoughtful, tapping a pen against his knuckle. He made a mental note to circle back later, just in case.

Chapter 19

The path curled along the lake like a ribbon dropped in slow motion. Autumn leaves flickered in the breeze—reds, oranges, the brittle yellow of dry grass. The late sun stretched through the trees, making long shadows across the asphalt.

Paige walked with her hands shoved deep in her hoodie pocket, head down, boots crunching leaf litter. She'd needed space, room to think, or maybe just room to feel without anyone watching. The stillness of the lake helped. So did the memory of quieter times.

She'd brought Yu-Chen here once or twice, but he couldn't sit still. Couldn't stop scanning the water like it held formulas. David, though, had always slowed down. Back then, this place had meant something.

She passed a picnic table and lowered herself onto the bench, heavy as stone. Nearby, a family folded their blanket, wrangled a child into sneakers. They waved as they passed. Paige managed a nod but kept her eyes down. She didn't want them to see her break.

She dropped her head into her arms. And this time the tears came hard, sudden, like a storm she couldn't outrun. Grief, guilt, relief, all tangled. The dam she had built since morning finally cracked, her shoulders slumping under the weight of it.

"Paige?"

She jerked upright, blinking into the sun.

David stood a few feet away on the path. Shocked. Cautious. Familiar.

She dragged a hand across her face. "What are you doing here?"

"I needed to clear my head," he said quietly. "I didn't expect to find you."

She pushed to her feet, already turning, legs moving before she could find words.

"Wait." His voice followed. "I heard about the engagement."

She froze.

"I saw Mr. Huang this morning. He told me."

Her jaw tightened. "Of course he did. This town." A brittle laugh escaped her. "Everyone's a damn newswire."

David didn't answer.

She turned back, sat down again, hugging herself like she had to hold in all the loose, breaking pieces. After a beat, David sat too, close but not touching.

"I'm sorry," he said. "I didn't come to make this harder."

She didn't reply at first, just stared at the water. The lake was calm, mirror-bright, but she felt hollow inside, scattered as broken glass.

He turned toward her. "Why'd you break it off?"

Her breath hitched. Words felt sharp in her throat.

"Because I wasn't in love with him." She squeezed her arms tighter around herself. "God, I wanted to be. I tried. He's a good man. He is patient, kind, smarter than I'll ever be. He never gave me a single reason not to love him. But every time I looked ahead, it felt like I was living someone else's life. Smiling on cue, saying yes because it was easier than asking what I really wanted." Her voice wavered. "And what I wanted... it wasn't him. No matter how much I wished it could be."

The silence after was thick, aching. The water lapped at the shore, a steady heartbeat against the quiet. A rower passed out in the channel, oars dipping rhythmically, the sound carrying thin in the afternoon air.

David let it settle between them, then spoke.

"I won't sign the contract."

Her head snapped around. "What?"

His hands clenched on his knees. "I won't join Doctors Without Borders. I'll walk away from the whole thing—whatever it costs."

"Are you serious? No, David. Don't put that on me. I won't be the reason you throw your future away."

"I don't care. I want to stay. With you."

"We already tried that, David. And it wrecked us. I'm not doing it again."

He reached for her hand. "Then let me try again. Don't walk away from me."

She stood up abruptly. "Your timing is crap."

He followed, reached out, and wiped a tear from her cheek. She didn't pull away.

They stood beneath a canopy of fiery orange leaves. The wind kicked up leaves around their feet. Their lips met—slow at first, then certain. Something old flared up between them, something unfinished.

"Paige?"

They broke apart. Paige turned.

Yu-Chen stood ten feet away, clutching the envelope that contained his letter. The one where he requested the autopsy, risked everything, just to prove he still believed her.

And here she was.

Kissing his best friend.

His face stayed blank, but his eyes, his eyes told the truth. Hurt, raw and unguarded, staring straight through her.

"Yu-Chen—" Paige stepped forward, words failing.

"I was looking for you," he said. His voice was controlled, almost too even.

Then, to David: "Med school wasn't enough, huh? You had to take her too?"

David flinched. "It's not like that. I swear—"

Yu-Chen's gaze cut back to Paige. "I thought you were done making me compare myself to him."

Yu-Chen turned and walked back toward the trail, the envelope still clutched in his hand.

Paige stood frozen. Then she turned on David.

"Oh God. I broke his heart. Again!"

"You didn't plan this," he said.

"No. But I sure as hell didn't stop it either."

She backed away, trying to breathe. "I need to go."

"Paige—"

She didn't look back.

The trail curved ahead of her, winding through the trees like it could lead somewhere better.

Chapter 20

Doctor Hyde cut into the last bite of his rare steak, the meat pink and glistening. Beyond the country club's floor-to-ceiling glass, soft amber patio lights shimmered against stone pillars wrapped in dormant vines. The golf course fell away into rolling hills, the distant rooftops bathed in the final glow of sunset. From here, Folsom looked tame. Manageable.

The waiter cleared Hyde's plate without a word.

Then, footsteps. Fast. Heavy.

A man in a trim Brioni suit appeared, winded, clutching a phone. Randall, Hyde's corporate attorney, scanned the dining room like he expected armed guards. He spotted Hyde and made a beeline.

Hyde didn't rise. He sipped his wine, expression unreadable.

"Randall," he said, "shouldn't you be at the office fending off the next class-action lawsuit? Or is this your cardio hour?"

Randall leaned in, still catching his breath. "Sir, we just received notice. Rosenberg and Associates filed dissolution paperwork. Effective yesterday."

Hyde set down his glass, very slowly. "He filed?"

Randall cleared his throat. "Yu-Chen Huang is now listed as the sole inventor of *Project Regenesis*."

Hyde didn't answer. So Yu-Chen thought it was over. Filed behind his back. Locked him out of the research.

But he was wrong.

Hyde's jaw tightened.

For a long moment, Hyde didn't move.

The hills darkened outside the window. The clubhouse lights buzzed to life.

Then, without a word, Hyde stood and adjusted his collar.

"Do you want me to follow up—?" Randall asked.

But Hyde was already gone, sliding past tables of diners too polite or too wary to stare.

A waiter approached with the check. Randall sighed, took it, and muttered, "Of course."

Outside, the glass door swung shut behind Doctor Hyde as he disappeared into the descending dark.

The parking lot was mostly empty, edges swallowed by trees and the hush of evening. Crickets chirped; patio lights flickered in the distance behind Hyde as he strode to his red Porsche, the kind of car that turned heads and brought a ghost of a smirk to his face.

He slid behind the wheel and hit speed dial, jaw tight.

A mile down the road, a black-and-white cruiser rolled past the country club gates. White clocked Hyde's red Porsche under the lamplight but said nothing. The patrol continued through dim shopfronts and streetlamps bleeding halos. Inside, White slouched in the driver's seat, whistling a tuneless refrain. Jamal, riding shotgun, reviewed call logs on the center console.

White's phone buzzed. He peeked at the screen, then answered with forced cheer.

"Hi Mom. Can't talk now."

Hyde's voice was cold, sharp. "Drop the games, Mike. You know what you need to do. Tonight."

White's grip tightened on the wheel. "Can't, remember? Chief's got me on a ride-along with Jamal. That hungry rookie I told you about? Kid's a real go-getter. You know how it is—public image, mentoring, all that."

He shot Jamal a grin, a little too wide. Jamal looked at him, eyes narrowing.

Hyde's reply was flat, impatient. "No more excuses. If things aren't fixed by morning, we both lose."

White's voice was clipped. "I can't see you tonight, Mom."

Hyde's voice cut through, low and dangerous: "If things go sideways, the chief will find a fat envelope on his doorstep by midnight."

White's lips thinned. "Sure, I'll call you next week."

A beat. Hyde: "You know what's on the line, Mike. Don't disappoint me."

White forced a laugh. "Love you too, Mom," and stabbed 'end call' with his thumb, pulse racing.

Jamal eyed him, half a smile. "Interesting family call."

White snorted. "She worries."

Jamal arched a brow. "I thought your mom was in memory care, down south?"

White's jaw tightened, fingers drumming the wheel. "You hear wrong sometimes, rookie."

Before Jamal could press, the radio crackled to life.

"Unit One, Mrs. Giuseppe's poodle is loose again. Corner of Third and Maple," Desk Sergeant Helga said, bored.

With relief, White grabbed the mic. "Unit One en route."

"Try not to lose the rookie or the poodle," Helga deadpanned.

White punched the cruiser into gear, welcoming the distraction as Jamal watched him a moment longer, thoughtful.

Back in the quiet parking lot, Hyde's Porsche idled, taillights burning against the dark.

He scrolled through contacts, thumb hovering over one name: Snake.

Not yet. Snake was for real cleanup—a last resort—no subtlety, just chaos.

Hyde exhaled. White was slipping, tangled up in nerves and alibis. But there was still time. If not, then Snake was next. And once Snake was in play, there'd be no dialing him back.

Hyde shut off the phone and watched the lot, engine rumbling low beneath his skin. For now, White had one more chance.

But nothing lasts forever.

Chapter 21

The string lights on the far wall cast a soft, amber glow—shadows gathered in the corners. Paige sat slumped on the edge of the couch, still in jeans and a hoodie, the patterned rug cool beneath her bare feet.

Her cell phone lay beside her, screen dark. She stared at it a moment, then tapped her screen and hit redial.

"Yu-Chen, will you please pick up?" Her voice cracked. "I'm sorry about earlier. It wasn't supposed to happen. Just... call me. Please."

She ended the call and dropped the phone onto the cushion beside her like it had burned her hand. She buried her face in her hands, then exhaled hard and leaned back.

A knock at the front door snapped her upright.

She crossed the small front hall, lit by the amber glow of the hanging lantern, its soft light pooling on the woven rug. Shadows stretched over the bench and leafy plants as she peered through the glass.

David stood on the porch.

She didn't open the door right away.

Finally, she unlatched it.

"David, not tonight."

"Paige, I won't stay long. I just need to say something face-to-face."

She stepped aside.

He walked in, taking in the quiet living room—soft lighting, the knitted throw draped across the couch, the tension clinging to the air like smoke.

David stayed standing.

"I only came to say I'm sorry," he said. "I shouldn't have kissed you."

She crossed her arms. "Great. You said it. Now go."

"I just wanted five minutes. Five minutes to say the one thing I never got to before you left."

"I said go."

He stepped back, jaw tight. "Fine. I'll take the DWB assignment. I won't come near you again. But before I go, you need to hear this. I should've said it back then. I should've told you I loved you when it mattered. But I never stopped, Paige. Not for a single day."

That landed like a punch.

She blinked hard, but a tear slid free anyway.

Suddenly she was back three years, knees pulled up beside him in the med school quad, listening to rain pound the library windows; the way David knew how to make her laugh when everything else felt like disaster. She'd built whole walls after that. Walls Yu-Chen had never quite scaled.

David froze. Then he moved.

He crossed the room in three steps, cupped her face, and brushed away the tear with his thumb.

"Don't—" she whispered.

But then his lips were on hers. Gentle at first. Testing.

She didn't stop him.

The kiss deepened. Her fingers curled into his jacket. He held her like he'd been starving for this, for her.

Her breath hitched.

"What are we doing?" she whispered.

***

The cottage felt too quiet, too heavy with memories he could not face—not after what happened with Paige. Yu-Chen lay on the couch, pulled a thin blanket over his shoulders, and let the hum of the lab equipment press him down. Just an hour, he thought. He switched off the light. Sleep closed in.

Outside the locked door, a gloved hand slid a keycard into the reader. A sharp beep broke the silence, then the lock clicked. The intruder slipped inside, black hood pulled low, mask and gloves concealing every trace. Rubber soles softened each step. He moved with simple control, letting the room dictate his path.

The lab smelled of metal and ethanol. Screens glowed pale. Shadows pushed across benches lined with glassware. He crouched, swept through notebooks and scattered printouts, and shoved the bundles straight into his pack. He didn't pause to study a page. He took what looked valuable, anything marked, anything near the edge.

A shift of air broke the stillness.

Yu-Chen stirred on the couch, blinking blearily. "Who's there?" His voice quivered between sleep and panic.

For a moment, no one spoke. Only the machines hummed.

Yu-Chen bolted upright. He ran for the door. His phone already clutched in his hand. His thumb stabbed the screen. Numbers lit: 9–1–1.

The intruder lunged. His hand crushed over Yu-Chen's mouth, the two slamming against the desk. A folder spilled across the floor, papers sliding out in a fan.

Desk Sergeant Helga's voice crackled out from the speaker: "Folsom Police Station. What is your emergency?"

A flash of blue slipped free from the intruder—small, hard, spinning light. The sapphire struck tile and vanished into shadow beneath a coil of cables. Neither man saw it fall.

"Hello?" Helga called from the phone. "If this is a damn prank—"

He fought hard, nails digging, heels hammering. The intruder forced an arm across his throat, pinning him until his kicking slowed, his grip faltered, and his eyes clouded. Yu-Chen's face flushed, his limbs jerking until they weakened, softened, sagged to the floor.

The intruder reached down, pressed the call off. But not fast enough.

"We've traced this line. Units en route."

The intruder stilled. His pack hung half-open, papers bleeding onto the floor. No time. The search was finished.

His gaze snapped to the open emergency cabinet. Vials gleamed inside, labels sharp under fluorescent light. He seized one and a syringe, yanked Yu-Chen's limp hand forward, clamped it tight on the barrel, and drove the needle into his arm. The plunger sank. Veins darkened. Yu-Chen jolted once, then went still. The syringe slipped from those same fingers and clattered across tile.

The intruder zipped the pack in one jerk and slung it over his shoulder. Sirens swelled, faint and closing. He cast one final sweep across the chaos: papers scattered, Yu-Chen's body slack on the floor.

He turned for the door.

Beneath a coil of wires, something small lay where it had fallen in the struggle. A sapphire stone, bright against the dark, rested unseen, waiting.

The intruder vanished into the night, leaving behind a half-stripped lab, a silenced call, a body, and the sound of sirens rushing closer.

***

"What are we doing?" Paige whispered.

David didn't answer. He kissed her again—longer, slower, full of history and heat.

His hands framed her face, thumbs brushing her cheekbones like she was something precious. She melted into him, her heartbeat tripping, breath catching as he pulled her even closer. His mouth moved over hers with a reverence that undid her.

"I walked away once, and it was a mistake. Let me make it right."

The phone buzzed again from the couch.

She pulled away, heart pounding. "No. We can't do this to Yu-Chen."

Buzz.

She grabbed the phone.

"Yu-Chen?..." Her voice caught. "Oh, Helga. I can't talk right now, I—"

Helga's voice was quiet. Careful.

"Paige... something's happened."

Paige froze.

"What?"

The air thinned. Her knees nearly buckled.

Chapter 22

Two squad cars sat at crooked angles outside the sleek glass facade of Black Core Labs, their light bars spinning in silence, painting the pavement red and blue. The night air buzzed with tension. Officer Jamal kept bystanders behind taped barricades.

Near the corner, Officer Garcia stood beneath a streetlamp, jotting notes as he questioned a jogger.

A green Subaru screeched into the curb. Before the wheels fully stopped, Paige flung the door open and sprinted toward the tape. David hardly had time to kill the engine before leaping out after her.

"Paige, wait!" he shouted.

She didn't. Her boots hit the pavement hard as she shoved past the tape. "Where is he?" she called out, voice rising. "Where's Yu-Chen?"

Garcia turned at the sound of her voice. "Jamal, take over," he snapped, then stepped forward. "Paige. You need to sit—"

She pushed past him. "No! Where is he?" Her eyes searched the lobby windows, wild and wide. "Is he alive? Tell me he's alive!"

"Paige, listen—"

But she was already at the building's glass doors, pounding once, then twice.

"Paige! You can't go in there!" Garcia barked, voice sharp now.

David reached him, breath short. "Officer Garcia. Please. What happened? Is he okay?"

Garcia looked at David. His mouth tightened. He didn't speak.

That silence said everything.

Paige froze against the glass, one hand splayed across the door. Her chest rose and fell in ragged bursts. She couldn't move. Couldn't breathe.

"Yu-Chen..." she whispered.

Behind her, a sharp crack came from the barricade. Someone shouting. A pedestrian broke through the tape. Garcia turned, barking orders. When he spun back—

Paige was already inside.

Flashing red-and-blue lights from squad cars streak across the glass. Paige bursts through the main doors, heart pounding. She slams the elevator button. Nothing. Locked.

She bolts for the stairwell, boots hammering the concrete steps.

Down the dim hallway, crime scene tape shivered at the edge of the lab door. Inside: pale fluorescents flickered, machines droned in steady rhythm. Yu-Chen's workstation glowed, a document frozen on-screen. A white sheet covered the figure on the floor.

Paige skidded into the lab.

"Yu-Chen!" Her voice tore down the room. "No. No—no!"

White turned from the body. "Paige, stop—"

She broke past him. He caught her in his arms, iron tightening against her ribs, but she fought him, thrashing against his chest, tears streaking her face.

"He's not dead! Let me see him!"

"Paige, you can't," White said, voice edged with strain.

She tore free, dropped to her knees, and clutched the sheet. She pulled it back an inch, just enough to see his face.

His lips parted like he had been caught mid-sentence. Hair still damp at the temples. He never toweled it dry. She used to tease him about it. She pressed trembling fingers to the edge of the sheet, trying to steady her breath.

"Why didn't you call me?" she whispered to him. "Why didn't you say goodbye?"

White's spoke low into his lapel mic. "I need a grief counselor down here. Now."

He reached forward, not rough but unyielding, and covered Yu-Chen again.

"Come on," he said. "Not here."

Paige didn't move. She smoothed the sheet flat, once, twice, her hands refusing stillness.

Garcia rushed in, breath quick, one hand still on the radio clipped to his vest. He scanned the scene. Paige crouched at the body. White standing over her. His face tensed. "Everything alright in here?"

Her head lifted. "What happened?"

"You need to go home," White said, his eyes shifting away. "You're too close to this.

"It was Hyde," she said. "You know it."

White's jaw tightened. "Paige, this was a suicide."

"No. This isn't him. It's staged."

"You're grieving. Let us handle it."

"You're damn right I'm grieving," she snapped, her voice gaining force. "But I'm not blind."

Her hand braced on the floor. A flash caught her eye. Near the cables, half-hidden by a fallen page, something glimmered. She leaned closer.

A stone. Sapphire, deep blue against the lab's pale tile.

She froze, her breath snagging. She reached toward it, stopped short, her hand poised above it.

"That's not his," she whispered. The recognition cracked through: the bookshop engagement party, Hyde's smirk under the lights, sapphire cufflinks winking handed over the red envelope.

Her voice sharpened. "That's Hyde's. He was here."

White stiffened. "Step back, Paige. Don't touch it."

"I don't need to," she said. "I know what it means."

Garcia strode in, crouched, and caught the sapphire with a gloved hand. He sealed it into a clear bag, then looked up, his brow knotted. White didn't answer; his gaze stayed locked on Paige.

The elevator chimed. The doors slid open.

Hyde stepped out first, Snake just behind him. Hyde's face wore concern like a mask.

"Is it true?" he asked. "Yu-Chen..."

"You son of a bitch."

Paige spun. Her fist cracked against his nose. Hyde staggered backward, blood pouring down his lip.

White lunged and caught her arms. "Paige!"

She strained in his grip, voice rising. "You killed him! He saw through you. He was ending the partnership! And now I've got proof. Your precious sapphire stone. Right by his body. And now it's evidence, you bastard."

Hyde pressed a handkerchief to his nose. His smile was thin, cruel.

"Understandable. Grief distorts. I'll accept your apology next week."

She drove forward again. White locked his hold.

Jamal rushed in, panting from the stairs.

"Jamal get her out."

He looped her arm, dragged her toward the exit. Her voice rang across the lab as the stairwell door closed behind them.

"He was murdered. And I'm going to prove it."

Hyde straightened his jacket, lifted his collar, and flicked a final glance at White. Neither spoke.

Garcia worked in silence near the workstation, bent over loose papers, not looking up.

White broke the silence, clipped and cold. "You're done here. Leave."

Hyde stepped into the elevator, slid a silver key across the panel. The lights flickered alive. Ding.

He smiled through the blood dripping from his nose.

"Partnerships fracture. Cleaner for some than others."

The doors closed.

Snake lingered near the door, the faint curve of a smile tracing his mouth as if the chaos satisfied him. White showed nothing, his eyes fixed on the body under the sheet, unreadable as stone.

Chapter 23

Yu-Chen bolted upright and lunged for the door.

The intruder cut him off, one hand clamped over his mouth, driving him back into the desk. A folder burst open, pages scattering across the floor.

A flash of blue spun free—hard, cold, sapphire light. It rattled once across tile, then slipped beneath the wires. Neither man saw it fall.

Yu-Chen clawed, heels pounding. The intruder's arm pressed across his throat, forcing him down. His legs kicked, slowed, stilled. Eyes rolled, body sagged.

The emergency cabinet yawned open. Glass vials gleamed in the light. The intruder snatched one, drew a syringe, and forced Yu-Chen's limp hand tight around the barrel. The needle sank. The plunger drove home. Yu-Chen jerked, then went still. The syringe slipped from his fingers and clattered to the floor.

The masked figure leaned close. Fingers pulled the hood back, tugged the mask free.

Hyde's calm face stared out. Watching the body, his lips curled in faint satisfaction.

Paige jolted awake, tears streaking down her temples. Her chest throbbed, hollow. Sunlight spilled through gauzy curtains, striping the living room in hard bands of gold.

She sat upright on the couch, a knitted throw tangled around her legs, her hoodie bunched at the neck. The pillows were crushed flat, evidence of a night lost to twisting dreams.

The silence pressed in like a second skin. Even the refrigerator hum felt muffled.

In the bathroom, she splashed cold water on her face, but the heaviness clung. She opened the mirrored cabinet for aspirin. Shut it.

Yu-Chen stood behind her.

"Help me, Paige."

The bottle slipped from her hand. Pills skittered across the floor like teeth shaken loose. She spun toward the doorway. Empty. Still air.

Her pulse hammered. She stumbled back to the living room, flung open the front door. Morning light poured in, almost too bright to look at. The street stretched silent, no footprints in the dew, no lingering voice.

Yu-Chen was gone. Or had never been there.

She leaned against the frame to keep standing. The month of the Hungry Ghost still burned through her mind, stories of spirits wandering the earth until someone guided them home. She pressed her forehead to her arm. "Just stress," she whispered. "Just... stress." The words broke in her throat. She didn't believe them.

Ever since her father left, Paige had believed there was a simple equation: disappoint someone you love, and they disappear. As a girl she'd blamed herself, and the verdict had stuck. Ending things with Yu-Chen, then that kiss with David in the park, only proved the rule in her mind—she only deserved love if she never failed the people she cared about.

She turned and drifted into the warm, inviting kitchen. Everything looked normal. Too normal. She opened the fridge. Pointless. She wasn't hungry.

That's when she saw it: a folded red napkin tucked behind a half-empty jar of pickles.

She pulled it out. Unwrapped it. Two almond cookies tumbled into her palm, Mrs. Chen's cookies.

The Hungry Ghost Festival. The spirits roam this month. Not a good night to walk alone, dear.

Paige stared at the cookies, her hands beginning to shake.

Help me.

She closed the fridge hard. The familiar warmth of the room felt wrong now, like stepping into a memory that wasn't hers.

She dropped the cookies on the floor, grabbed her keys and bolted.

She didn't know what she'd find.

But she knew where she had to go.

To Mrs. Chen.

Chapter 24

Up ahead, Mrs. Chen stepped out of the tea shop, a red pastry box tucked under one arm. Her free hand trembled as she slid the key into the lock. It slipped. The keys clattered to the sidewalk.

Paige hurried forward.

"Mrs. Chen!"

Mrs. Chen turned, her face crumpling at the sound of her name. "Oh, Paige..." They folded into a quiet embrace on the sidewalk, two women caught in the same storm.

"I was just closing up," Mrs. Chen murmured against her shoulder. "Harold can't even stand. I don't know how to help him. And you... poor girl..."

Paige bent to retrieve the keys. She pressed them into Mrs. Chen's hand.

"I need to ask you something. Something you said at the engagement party," Paige said.

Mrs. Chen blinked. "The party?" She frowned, searching her memory. "That feels like a lifetime ago."

She clutched the pastry box like it might steady her. "Last night, Officer Garcia came in person. Harold couldn't even speak. I've been shaking since."

She turned back to the door, trying again to lock it with one hand. Her voice filled the silence, more out of habit than intention.

"I wanted to be sure Minnie didn't open this morning. Didn't want to shoo away customers mid-weep. So, I came early, locked up. Thought I'd head to Harold's. We're meeting at the funeral home."

She paused, breath hitching.

"Harold wants a proper coffin. But Yu-Chen... Yu-Chen told us years ago he wanted to be cremated. Said he didn't want to waste the real estate." She tried for a smile, but it faltered.

"I got in the car, then realized I'd forgotten my jacket. Came back. But it's not here. Must've left it at home. Grief makes a mess of the mind. You forget everything, except the ache."

Her gaze settled on Paige. "What did you need to ask, dear?"

"It's about what you said. The Hungry Ghost Festival," Paige interrupted, voice taut. "The spirits roaming... was that a metaphor, or did you mean it?"

Mrs. Chen froze. Her gaze sharpened. "Paige... you saw something."

Paige didn't answer.

Inside the shop, the air carried traces of jasmine and rose, soft as memory. Tufted velvet chairs and mismatched floral upholstery flanked a patchwork of antique rugs. Delicate china teapots lined the shelves like heirlooms. Amber light bathed the room, casting everything in a sepia glow. It felt less like a business and more like a sanctuary, a Victorian parlor preserved in time. Mrs. Chen moved on instinct, setting two porcelain cups on a carved table between the chairs. She clutched the teapot for a beat longer than necessary, her fingers tightening around the handle as if bracing herself.

From the spout of the teapot, steam rose in thin ribbons, like incense in a temple, like a ghost's breath.

"In our culture," Mrs. Chen said, pouring with steady hands, "the gates of the afterlife open this month. The dead may cross over, especially the restless. Hungry ghosts wander, craving, never full."

"Why are they hungry?" Paige asked, her eyes fixed on the twisting steam above her cup.

"Some are forgotten by their families. Others taken too soon. And some..." Mrs. Chen's gaze dropped to the table, "...are punished souls."

"Yu-Chen wasn't evil. And he won't be forgotten." Paige's voice wavered, then hardened. "Could there be another reason?"

Mrs. Chen's gaze sharpened. "Those who die violent deaths..." Her voice dipped. "...sometimes return. Not for food, but for justice."

Paige's breath caught. A flash of memory hit: the sapphire glinting on the lab floor, Hyde's cufflinks at the engagement party. Murder. She felt the words rise to her tongue. She was ready to tell her, ready to name, but she forced the words back.

The silence stretched. Mrs. Chen reached across the table. "Paige... did Yu-Chen come to you?"

Paige kept her gaze down. "What do you mean?"

"You saw him, didn't you? Or heard him. He sent a message."

Paige shoved her chair back, the scrape harsh against tile. "I haven't been sleeping. I saw nothing. It was stress. A dream. That's all."

"Please. What did he say? Harold would want to know—"

"I imagined it," Paige said, her eyes burning. "I shouldn't have brought it up."

She turned for the door.

"Paige—wait—"

The bell above the frame chimed as she stepped into the glare outside. The street blurred with sunlight, old storefronts, and strangers' voices, a world that turned foreign beneath the weight in her chest. She kept walking, fists tight. Whatever came for her in the mirror that morning—ghost, memory, or worse—it had pleaded for help. And she would answer. Yu-Chen didn't choose death. Someone chose it for him. And she would not stop until she proved who.

***

In the breakroom, White filled his chipped mug, then stared at the brown liquid like it might blink first.

His eyes burned. Too much had gone sideways this week. Yu-Chen was dead, and the chief was ready to explode at any minute. And now Hyde was breathing down his neck. He rubbed his temples, trying to clear the fog.

From out in the bullpen, a voice cut through.

"Really? That's great, Garcia. I'll be there in twenty," said Jamal.

White stiffened. The mug in his hand felt heavier than it should. He stepped out of the break room, trying not to look like he was listening too closely.

Jamal was halfway into his jacket. Energy buzzed off him. Behind him, late sunlight streamed through the blinds, casting slatted shadows across the bullpen floor.

White crossed to his desk and dropped into his chair, swirling the last of his coffee.

"What's got you all lit up?"

Jamal grabbed his keys from the hook. "Garcia found a witness to the Gold Rush Museum break-in."

White's hand paused mid-sip. The mug hovered an inch from his mouth. "A witness?"

"Guy was out of town all week," Jamal said, energized. "Just got back. Saw something near the back alley the night it happened. Might've caught a plate."

White lowered the mug, but too carefully. He set it down with silent precision, then adjusted it like it mattered. "You're not going."

Jamal blinked. "Come again?"

"I said Garcia's got it. He's the lead. Let him handle it."

"You serious right now?"

White rose, heading to his desk. His tone stayed level. But his movements sharpened—papers stacked, pens aligned, as if staying busy might hold him together. "Still his case. And the witness might spook easy. Garcia's building trust."

Jamal frowned. "Since when do you give a damn about witness rapport?"

Helga wandered in, tearing open a powdered creamer. "God forbid we scare off the one person in this town who saw something worth reporting."

White shot her a look, brief, flat, and just sharp enough to make her go quiet.

Jamal's gaze stayed fixed. "Look, if you've got a reason I shouldn't assist, say it."

White didn't blink. "No reason. Just follow the chain of command."

Jamal studied him for a beat too long, then slowly rehung his jacket.

"Sure," he said. "Chain of command."

But his eyes said something else.

Chapter 25

Paige dug out her phone and dialed Jamal, clutching it to her ear as she passed the faded brick and painted trim of Sutter Street. Voicemail. Her voice shook, but she forced the words out:

"Jamal, it's Paige. Call me the second you get this. Has anyone found out anything about that sapphire from the lab? Please, I need to know."

A few doors down, Mr. Peterson stepped out of his antique shop. He flipped his sign to CLOSED and locked the door, a bank pouch tucked under his arm. As he turned, he overheard Paige ending her call.

He gave a small wave. "Afternoon, Officer Gold. You sounded urgent."

She tucked her phone away and crossed over, exhaustion softening her guard. "Sorry, Mr. Peterson. Just work. What's up?"

He lowered his voice. "Not to pry, but I overheard you mention a sapphire. Odd thing—someone came in this week with a stone for sale. The sapphire itself, deco cut, expensive, wrapped in tissue paper like it was nothing. That's the kind of stone you'd expect in a vault, not passed across a shop counter."

Paige's pulse jumped. "Can you describe him? Did you get a name?"

Mr. Peterson nodded. "Tall, broad-shouldered. Bald. Moved like he was used to making people nervous. He had the stone in a pouch, didn't want to say where he got it. When I asked for ID and proof of ownership, he got cagey—left right away."

As he described the visitor, Paige drifted, images rising unwanted:

Yu-Chen kicked, gasping, the intruder's arm pinning him down, the glint of the syringe. In her mind, the masked figure bent, hands pulling away the hood, the mask slipping free.

Snake's face looked back. Pale, unreadable. A hint of satisfaction curled his lip as he watched Yu-Chen die.

"Paige?" Mr. Peterson's voice snapped her back. "Are you alright? You looked miles away."

She blinked, fighting to steady herself. "If that man comes back, call me right away. Please."

Without waiting for an answer, she turned and headed toward the corner, heart pounding. The ghost in her dreams, the stone in her memory, Snake's face. None of it would let her go.

***

Paige slipped in through the station's back entrance, letting the door fall shut behind her. In the bullpen, Jamal scanned a report, Helga sorted forms, White hunched over a case file.

At the far end, the Chief's office door was closed most of the way. Through the glass and drawn blinds, she saw two silhouettes—one standing, one seated—layers of blinds striping the room. Paige kept to the hallway, head down, and moved to the locker room.

She pushed through the door into the women's locker area: tight space, metal lockers scuffed and dented, a single bench running the length. Her reflection ghosted back at her from a battered locker door.

She suited up, duty shirt buttoned, belt cinched. Closing her locker, she set her jaw and strode out, braced for what came next.

The blinds cast harsh stripes of light across Chief Jones' office, slicing through the stale air like warning lines. Certificates and commendations lined the wall behind his desk—silent witnesses to decades of service and split-second decisions. His sleeves were rolled past the elbows, sweat darkening the creases at his shoulders. He didn't sit. He stood behind the desk like a boulder, bracing for an avalanche.

Across from him, Randall Cohen set down a leather-bound folder with a thud that felt rehearsed. His suit clung to him like a shell. The man didn't sweat. He smirked.

"My client will not pursue litigation," Randall said, "if Officer Gold agrees to a formal apology to Doctor Hyde."

Jones didn't flinch. "On behalf of the department, tell Hyde we regret the situation escalated. I'm sure Gold will cooperate."

The door burst open before Randall could respond.

Paige stormed in, in uniform, eyes fierce.

"What's going on?"

Jones turned, anger flickering behind his eyes. "Paige, I told you to stay home."

Randall folded his arms. "Ms. Gold, my client is filing suit for physical assault, emotional trauma, and damage to reputation. One million dollars in damages, pending escalation."

"He's an asshole, and you know it."

"Officer Gold," Jones warned, voice low, steel-cored.

Randall didn't miss a beat. "We're prepared to file within the hour. Every delay increases the cost of settlement. Also, Dr. Hyde insists on a televised apology. Tonight."

Paige's mouth twisted in disbelief. "Is this a joke?"

"Enough," Jones barked. "Apologize. You were in shock, you lashed out. It happens. But this? This is bigger than you."

"No," Paige said. "Apologize to that bastard? Never."

Randall straightened. "Then we'll proceed with the lawsuit."

"Get the hell out," Paige said.

Randall didn't blink. He buttoned his jacket, turned to Jones. "You have my number."

Paige shut the door behind him.

Beyond the glass, the bullpen froze. Helga hovered over her keyboard. Jamal leaned back from his screen. White shifted in his chair, then looked away.

Jones rubbed his temples, then lowered himself into his seat. The room felt tighter now, like the walls were closing in.

"Paige," he said, voice gravel low. "I'm trying to protect you. And this department."

"Hyde isn't a victim." Her voice cut like glass. "He wanted Yu-Chen's cure. Killed him for it."

Jones straightened, eyes flaring. "Christ. Don't go there."

"Yu-Chen ended their deal. Hyde got desperate."

Jones shook his head. "You're not thinking clearly."

"I'm the only one who is. And Hyde can kiss my ass. I'll say *that* on live TV."

Jones stood, both hands braced on the desk. "You're grieving. I get it. But this is bigger than you. You assaulted a civilian with a team of lawyers behind him. Will you apologize?" His voice dropped, cold as steel. "And think hard before you answer."

She didn't flinch. "No."

He held her stare. Then exhaled. "Badge and weapon, Gold."

Paige unpinned her badge. Set it on the desk. The metal clicked against the wood. Then she drew her sidearm, placed it beside it, and stepped back.

"I'll find the truth," she said. "With or without a badge."

Jones didn't reply. He only nodded once.

She walked out.

In the bullpen, every officer looked up. Then quickly looked away.

Jones watched her leave through the blinds, his reflection dim in the glass.

Then, alone in the silence, he slammed his palm on the desk.

"Goddamn it."

He opened his door and stepped into the silence.

"Get back to work."

Chairs squeaked. Keyboards clicked. No one met his eye.

Chapter 26

Soft light filtered through the blinds, striping the sleek white walls. The desk gleamed, everything neat except for the restless tapping of David's fingers beside his cell phone.

"Dr. David Lau, Folsom Valley Clinic," he said into the receiver. "I'm trying to reach whoever handled Yu-Chen Huang's autopsy... yes, I'll hold."

He exhaled hard, eyes fixed on the framed medical degrees hanging on the wall above his computer. The hold music crackled. Then—

"Hello? Dr. Murphy? Thanks for taking my call. I wanted to confirm—were you the pathologist assigned to Huang's case?"

Just outside the doorway, Nurse Naomi Jenkins paused. The door hung open a few inches, enough for her to see David inside, pacing, his shoulders tight. She lifted a hand to knock... then hesitated.

David turned toward the bookshelf, lowered his voice. "Before the death certificate is finalized, I need to ask, were there signs of trauma? Bruising? Anything unusual?"

A beat of silence.

"No, I'm not family. But I was his friend. His closest one." He blinked hard. "I understand protocol, but your office has always been... cooperative. I've never been shut out like this before."

He stopped dead in his tracks.

"The police won't release anything. Not even the time of death." His jaw tensed. "Is someone leaning on your office?"

Another pause. Then his voice fell flat. "I see. Thank you, Dr. Murphy."

He ended the call. Stared at the screen. Then murmured under his breath, "Damn it."

A knock at the door.

Nurse Jenkins stepped in, her expression soft but grounded. "Sorry, Dr. Lau. Mrs. Giuseppe's waiting. Her arthritis is giving her more pain."

David straightened, smoothing his coat like armor. "Thanks. I'll be right there."

He moved past her toward the hallway, masking the storm under his usual calm.

Nurse Jenkins glanced at the phone still glowing on his desk, then at the man disappearing down the corridor.

She shook her head.

"Something's not right," she murmured and followed David down the hall.

The fluorescent lights flickered above the narrow hallway of Valley Clinic, casting long, pale reflections across the linoleum floor. Through the sliver of light beneath exam room three, David's voice drifted out, calm and clinical.

"Mrs. Giuseppe, how are you feeling today?"

Nurse Jenkins clicked the door shut behind them.

In the corridor, shadows deepened. At the far end two shapes appeared.

Charlie came first, his edges shifting, smoke over hot asphalt. Yu-Chen followed; his form held together by the ache of what he left behind. He stared at the closed door.

"Bro," Charlie muttered, leaning against the wall or trying to. His shoulder sank through it. "You've got people in your corner, I'll give you that. But that autopsy? County doc signed off before the ink dried. Suicide, no bruises, no questions. Just how the bastards wanted it."

Yu-Chen's hands curled into fists. "Doctor Murphy isn't the bastard. He must've been pressured."

"Sure. Doesn't change the outcome."

"Paige will see this through. For both of us."

Charlie scoffed, the sound thin in the air. "But come on, man. They kicked her to the curb. She's got no badge, no voice."

He paused, watching Yu-Chen's face.

"But she's still digging, isn't she? That girl doesn't let go. She'll find the cracks. The dude won't see her coming."

Yu-Chen's voice was low. "You don't know what that man is capable of."

"I know what *she's* capable of," he said. "She's got grit, that one. Fire in her gut. She walked into that lab like she owned the place."

Yu-Chen looked away, jaw clenched tight. Fear and hope twisted inside him, twin knives.

Charlie's voice softened. "You trust her. That's all you can do. Me too."

Charlie glanced down the corridor, where the shadows stretched farther than they should. "Festival ends tonight." He paused, the words heavy. "After this, the gate closes. No more crossing over. No more borrowed time. Just the dark.

Yu-Chen swallowed. "She'll finish it.

"And if she can't?"

Yu-Chen didn't answer. He fixed his eyes on the door, the living world just out of reach.

Charlie let out a shudder. "Yeah. Thought so."

Behind them, the last bulb hummed and burned steady, but a different darkness gathered between the walls, pressing the ghosts into silence and leaving pain in its wake.

Chapter 27

Back in the locker room, Paige ripped off her uniform and tossed it into her bag. She threw on jeans and a faded T-shirt, anger fueling every move. Her phone buzzed. Callahan's name lit the screen. She grabbed it, pulse kicking.

"Detective Callahan, thanks for calling. Is this about the sapphire case?"

He sounded surprised, then grateful. "Right. That's the one. We tracked down Giuseppe, the owner of that old rental agency. The mom-and-pop shop got swallowed by a chain, but the big company lost access to all the rental records from before the merger. Giuseppe's memory isn't great, but he kept paper files for taxes. Right now, he's at his storage locker, digging for anything that might help."

She didn't hesitate. "I know Mr. Giuseppe. Text me the address of the storage unit."

Callahan hesitated a beat. "Make sure he doesn't misfile or toss anything important. If you find the renter's license copy, lock it down. We need that sapphire, Paige."

For the first time in days, hope broke through Paige's exhaustion. The copy of the driver's license might lead straight to the man who killed Yu-Chen.

"I'm on my way now."

Callahan waited a beat. "Keep him focused. If he finds the renter's license, don't let it out of your sight. That slip could break the whole case open."

She ended the call and charged for the exit, hope driving her faster than the sting of a lost badge.

Paige pulled into the storage facility on the edge of town. Rows of red metal doors stretched across the asphalt under the afternoon sun. She parked and crossed the empty lot, her footsteps echoing between the low concrete buildings.

Giuseppe's storage unit stretched back like a narrow cave, boxes stacked floor to ceiling in precarious towers. Purple and blue plastic bins wedged between cardboard boxes marked with faded ink. The air hung thick with dust and the musty smell of old paper. Loose documents carpeted the floor where Giuseppe had pulled them from various containers.

Giuseppe wore a button-down shirt and jeans, too heavy for the heat. Sweat beaded on his forehead as he shuffled between scattered boxes, his thin fingers trembling slightly. Papers and photo albums lay open on the concrete floor, abandoned mid-search.

"Mr. Giuseppe! Hello again."

He looked up, blinking. "I'm sorry, you are?"

"Officer Paige Gold. I came to help you find that rental paperwork."

"Oh yes." He wiped his face with his sleeve. "That detective from San Francisco. I can't recall his name. He said you'd come. I'm afraid I'm no organizer. My Loretta handled all the books, but her arthritis flared up."

The storage unit trapped the heat like an oven. Dust motes swirled in the shaft of sunlight. Paige counted two dozen boxes marked with last year's date but no months. Her chest tightened.

She spotted a folding chair buried under loose papers. "Here, sit down. Let me handle the boxes. We need September of last year."

Giuseppe lowered himself into the chair. "My Loretta was the first female bookkeeper at Republic Insurance back in Owatonna. Blazed a trail for women in those days."

Paige tore into the nearest box. Inside were tax forms, receipts, contracts from three years back. Wrong pile. She moved to the next.

"Say, you're with the police department? I thought San Francisco was hours away, but you got here in no time."

"I'm from Folsom PD, Mr. Giuseppe." She swallowed. At least that wasn't a lie. Technically.

He stood and began pulling photo albums from another box. "What are we looking for again?"

"The rental agreement. Just rest. I'll find it."

Giuseppe closed several box lids, then reached for the last one. His eyes lit up as he peered into a manila folder. "Well, look at that! Found it!" His voice carried triumph, the satisfaction of completing a task.

Paige spun around from the box she was searching. Giuseppe clutched the folder against his chest, something white visible inside.

"Did you find it? The copy of the driver's license?" Paige couldn't hide the excitement in her voice.

Giuseppe blinked at her. The triumph on his face flickered, then faded like a candle in wind. He looked down at the folder in his hands, then back at her. What was he supposed to find again? The young woman's eyes sparkled with hope. She had hazel eyes, just like his dear Loretta's when she was young.

He tried to grasp the thread of what they'd been doing, but it slipped away like water through his fingers. "I... I know I've seen you around town. Aren't you the parking enforcement girl?"

Paige's throat tightened. "I work with the Folsom Police Department. Please, don't worry about the search. I can handle the boxes."

Giuseppe's phone buzzed somewhere in the mess. He searched under papers, found it, and answered.

"Loretta, how did the clinic go?... Now calm down, honey. I'm at the storage unit going through old boxes... Well, of course I drove myself... Don't be mad... I'm working on something important. Remember that detective from San Francisco who called earlier... You don't need to bother the grandkids... But I can drive home... Yes, okay, I'll leave the keys under the visor and wait for the Uber at the gate... Yes, sweetheart... I'll be home soon."

Paige cringed. The old man shouldn't be driving. His confusion was getting worse.

"I have to go. Loretta ordered me an Uber. Ten minutes. Can we try again tomorrow?"

"Mr. Giuseppe, I'll lock up. Just leave me the key and I'll drop it off at—"

The photocopy slipped from his fingers and fluttered to the concrete.

Her phone rang. Wise Huang's name flashed on screen. Her stomach dropped.

"Hello, Mr. Huang, I... What? ... What!"

Her knees buckled. She sank onto a stack of boxes, tears burning her eyes. "I'll be right there," she said wiping away a tear. She ended the call.

"I have to go." She choked on the words.

"Is everything all right, dear? You look upset."

She grabbed a scrap of paper from an open box and scrawled her number. "Text me and I'll come back tomorrow." She stuffed it into his jacket pocket.

Paige fled toward the parking lot, tears blurring her vision.

Behind her, Giuseppe turned off the unit's light. A breeze caught the paper, lifting it into the air. It drifted past his feet and out into the lot.

Giuseppe pulled the metal door down with a sharp clang that echoed between the buildings. He shuffled toward the entrance, muttering to himself. "Nice girl, that meter maid. Sharp as a tack. Could probably do more than write parking tickets if someone gave her the chance."

His phone chimed. The Uber waited at the entrance. He shuffled away.

The photocopy tumbled across the asphalt, caught the wind, and slapped against the building. For a moment, the image was clear: an alias name, but Mike White's face staring back.

Another gust lifted the paper and carried it toward the open field beyond the fence, where it disappeared into the tall grass.

Chapter 28

Paige parked her blue Impala beneath the sprawling oak that shaded Yu-Chen's cottage. She turned off the engine and gripped the steering wheel. The small blue house with white trim looked the same as always. Potted mums flanked the front steps, the oval glass door caught the afternoon light. Nothing had changed, yet everything had.

She walked to the front door, each step heavier than the last. Before she could knock, Wise Huang opened it.

"Thank you for—" His voice caught. He squared his shoulders, willing strength into his frame. "Please, come in."

The entrance hall felt smaller than usual, its warm wood floors and streaming sunlight unable to lift the weight pressing on her chest. She'd walked across this woven rug countless times. She'd rushed to meet Yu-Chen for dinner dates, bringing groceries for weekend cooking sessions, storming out just yesterday with her engagement ring abandoned on the console table. The simple bench against the wall still bore the jacket she'd forgotten last week, back when their biggest problem seemed to be wedding planning. The ring still rested on the dark console table, exactly where she'd left it, and Wise Huang's eyes stayed carefully away from it.

They moved into the living room, where exposed wooden beams stretched across the ceiling and built-in cabinets lined the walls. The kitchen opened seamlessly into the space, all warm wood and careful craftsmanship. Yu-Chen's laptop sat open on the dining table, screen glowing.

Wise Huang stood beside it, looking lost. "I came to... be close to him somehow. Wanted to put away his computer. Must not have shut down properly. Screen lit up right away when I touched it."

Paige stepped closer, her stomach dropping. Text filled the screen—a document, white letters against the blue background. Her eyes found the words before her mind could stop them:

My Dearest Paige,

I have reached the place where holding on serves neither of us. You deserve a life free of my burdens, a path I cannot walk beside you. Carry forward with your dreams and your joy.

Always,

Yu-Chen

The words hit her like a physical blow. All her certainty about the sapphire, about murder, about Hyde and Snake, it crumbled. Yu-Chen had chosen this. The note was there, on his own computer. She had been wrong about everything.

"I'm sorry," she whispered, tears blurring her vision. "I'm so sorry."

Wise Huang moved toward her, his arms opening. They held each other and wept—for Yu-Chen, for the future that would never come, for the questions that now had their terrible answer.

In her mind, Paige felt everything collapse at once. Her fiancé was gone by his own choice. Her career lay in ruins. Everyone would blame her because she drove him to this. The badge she'd worn with pride meant nothing now. The life she'd built, the future she'd planned, the love she'd believed in—all of it dissolved like salt in tears.

She clung to Wise Huang in the cottage that still smelled like Yu-Chen's coffee and books, surrounded by the life he'd chosen to leave behind.

Two blocks down Coloma Street, White sat in his black Tahoe, engine idling behind a sprawling wall of oleander. Pink blossoms carpeted the asphalt around his tires. Through the dense flowering branches, he watched the cottage's front door.

He pulled out his phone and hit speed dial. “It's done.”

Before Hyde could respond, White ended the call and shifted into drive. The Tahoe pulled away from the curb, leaving only scattered petals and tire marks on the quiet residential street.

Chapter 29

The sun dropped behind the trees, lengthening the shadows on David's old brick building. Paige jogged slow, sweat drying against her arms. She hadn't aimed for this street. She just needed to move until her head cleared.

The smell of grass. The faint ping of windchimes. The quiet hush of evening settling.

And then David.

He sat on a rock near the curb, shoulders bent. He looked up, surprised. "Paige?"

She stopped, breathing hard. "Didn't plan to end up here."

"That's a long run from your place."

She shrugged. "Couldn't stay home."

They walked without deciding to, side by side along the curb. Daylilies glowed orange in the fading light. Neither spoke. Her hand almost brushed his, but she pulled back.

He broke the silence. "I looked into Yu-Chen's file. They stonewalled me."

Her chest tightened. "So you tried."

"I did. But Paige..." David's voice grew careful. "What if we're wrong? What if—"

"Don't." The word came out sharp.

They stopped under a lamppost. David turned to her. "I know you need answers. But maybe the answer is the one we don't want to hear."

She stared at him. "You think he killed himself."

"I think he was in pain. Real pain. And maybe—"

"He wouldn't abandon his research. He wouldn't abandon me."

David's expression softened. "People in that kind of darkness... they don't see clearly. They think everyone's better off without them."

The words hit like a physical blow. Paige felt something crack inside her chest. it was the last wall holding back the truth she'd been fighting for days.

"I can't accept that," she whispered.

"I know."

A moving van idled down the street. David followed her gaze, then looked back at her. "I took the job. Doctors Without Borders."

The world tilted. "You're leaving."

"Six months. Maybe a year."

She stared at the van, at the boxes being loaded. Her last ally, walking away. The person who might have helped her keep fighting, gone.

"I need you to stay," she said, but her voice held no conviction.

"Paige—"

"No, I..." She stopped, the words dying. What was she fighting for? A theory no one believed? A case no one would investigate? A truth that might not exist?

The silence stretched between them.

"Maybe you're right," she said finally, the admission scraping her throat raw. "Maybe I've been seeing murder because I can't face the alternative."

David reached for her hand. "It doesn't make his pain less real. Or yours."

She pulled away. "If you're leaving, and I can't prove anything, and everyone thinks..." She swallowed hard. "Then what's the point of staying?"

"Paige—"

"I think I need to go too." The words surprised her, but once they were out, they felt true. "There's nothing left for me here."

David's face crumpled. "Don't leave because of me."

"I'm not." She looked around at the familiar street, the apartment complex, the life that suddenly felt like a shell. "I'm leaving because Yu-Chen's gone. And maybe he chose to go. And I can't... I can't keep pretending otherwise."

The admission hung in the air between them, final as a closing door.

David stepped toward her. "We don't have to say goodbye like this."

But Paige was already backing away, her decision crystallizing with each step. "Take care of yourself, David."

She turned and walked away, leaving him beneath the rattling windchimes, carrying the weight of a truth she was finally ready to stop fighting.

Chapter 30

The bullpen sat quiet in the blue hour before dawn. Only Jamal and White worked at their desks, fluorescent light sharpening the lines in their faces. Jamal looked up from his reports and caught White scrolling through files on his computer.

Jamal glanced at White's computer screen, catching glimpses of Garcia's report. "Saw Jenkins's statement about the SUV parked by the Gold Rush Museum. No plate, but Garcia's digging through camera feeds. With luck, they'll catch a shot of the driver."

White's hand froze over his mouse. "Cameras?"

"Yeah. Garcia's thorough like that." Jamal studied White's face. "Problem?"

"No problem." White's voice came out too quick. He turned back to his screen, jaw tight.

"Speaking of cases, there's a missing file from Paige's log. I overheard her talking to SFO PD about some rental car inquiry."

White's shoulders went rigid. "What kind of inquiry?"

"Detective tracking a rental car from a motel death. Dead prostitute was wearing jewelry from that armored car heist last year. They traced the rental to someone here in Folsom." Jamal watched White's reflection in the computer monitor. The man had gone pale. "Simple follow-up. I can handle it."

"I'll handle Paige's cases," White said, his words clipped and final.

Jamal frowned. "I've already started reviewing her files."

White didn't turn. "Go home, Jamal. I need space to sort this out."

Jamal grabbed his jacket, mind churning. White's reaction felt wrong. Too sharp. Too worried. "See you tomorrow, then."

Jamal walked down the hallway to the front doors. His suspicions crystallizing into something harder. White wasn't just being territorial about the cases.

He was covering something up.

***

The door to the bookshop jingled shut behind her.

Paige stepped onto Sutter Street, the morning sun washing the buildings in soft gold. Old Town looked almost like it did the day she arrived. Except everything had changed.

Amy waited on the sidewalk. She fell into step as Paige approached her car parked beneath the trees.

"How'd it go with Mr. Huang?" Amy asked.

Paige didn't answer right away. "He took it hard. But I have to do this."

Amy hesitated. "What if you just took a break? A long one. Came back when you were ready—"

"I'm not coming back." Paige pulled her house key from her backpack and pressed it into Amy's hand. "Put it on the market. As is. Furniture and all."

"This is all so sudden." Amy's voice cracked. "What can I do to change your mind?"

"You can't. But thank you."

Amy opened her mouth, then shut it again. "Where will you go?"

"I'll figure it out when I get there."

They hugged — hard and fast. Neither of them said the word goodbye.

The bell above the bookshop jingled again. Wise Huang stepped outside.

"Paige, wait," Wise Huang called, hurrying out of the shop.

She turned as he stepped out of the bookshop, crossing the short stretch of sidewalk with two books cradled in his arms, their covers catching the morning light.

"You left this one behind," he said, offering *Love Is the Ultimate Medicine*. "From the engagement party. "I thought you should keep it. There's another," he added after a pause, his fingers lingering on the second book, *The Elixir of Life: The Origins of Taoist Alchemy*.

He didn't release it right away. His thumb hovered at the spine, tracing a crease. "Yu-Chen gave it to me. But I can't keep it in the shop." His voice softened. "Every time I shelve it..." He stopped, shook his head. "They belong with family now."

Paige took the books, her hands brushing the worn covers. She nodded, throat tight. "Thank you."

Wise Huang studied her face for a long moment. "I wish you would stay. It's hard losing you both."

The words landed hard. Would he still say that if he knew? If he knew she kissed David, maybe at the very moment Yu-Chen took his last breath?

She blinked back the sting behind her eyes. "Goodbye, Mr. Huang." They hugged.

The bell jingled, a customer stepped inside. Wise Huang gave her a soft smile, squared his shoulders, and disappeared through the red doors.

Paige lingered a moment, then stepped out into the sunlit afternoon. The air smelled of roasted beans and warm pastries. Across the street, steam curled from the open window of a matte-blue coffee truck.

She crossed to her car, placed both books, *Love Is the Ultimate Medicine* and *The Elixir of Life,* gently on the passenger seat. Sunlight caught on the worn spines.

From the coffee truck window, a barista passed a cup to the man in the black suit. Hyde didn't drink coffee. But he needed a reason to be there when Paige came out. He reached into his pocket, pulled out his phone, and hit speed dial.

"It's me," he said. "Shut up, Mike. I don't care if you're on duty. We cleared out Yu-Chen's lab. But the last of the gold dust is still out there. Find it."

Hyde's grip tightened on the phone, knuckles blanching. Across the street, Paige's car glinted in the sun.

He ended the call, dropped the untouched coffee into the trash with a clatter, and strode off without looking back—coat crisp, jaw clenched, footsteps clipped. Time was slipping, and control with it.

Paige started the engine and pulled away from the curb, unaware of the gold flecks clinging to the books beside her.

Chapter 31

Miguel joined Amy on the sidewalk as she sadly watched Paige drive away and disappear down the road.

"There goes my best friend," said Amy.

Miguel and Amy walked down Sutter street past several quaint shops, heading to their tiny newspaper office.

"Amy, I have to ask. What if Yu-Chen didn't commit suicide. What if—"

"SHHHH! Someone will hear you." She motioned her head to the park next door. They quickly head over there and walked along a quiet path through the park.

"Miguel, don't ever say that in public again. It's dangerous."

"You mean because of Doctor Hyde? if it's true don't you think we should..."

"Investigate? Miguel this isn't some TV cop show. We could get sued for libel!"

"But Hyde had a motive. Paige said Yu-Chen dissolved their partnership on that miracle drug. That could have been worth billions."

Amy looked at Miguel. "Hyde may be unethical, but murder is a whole other thing. And he's not the type to get his hands dirty."

Across from the park, Hyde slipped behind a row of dumpsters and pulled out a black cufflink box. Its last remaining occupant a heavy gold cufflink crowned with a deep-blue sapphire, a perfect match for the stone found near Yu-Chen's body. For a moment, Hyde hesitated, jaw clenched in frustration at the loss. But he couldn't risk the connection. With one last glance for witnesses, he crouched by an old storm drain and flicked the cufflink inside. The sapphire caught a sliver of sunlight before vanishing into the darkness below. Hyde dropped the empty box into a trash bin, forcing himself to walk away.

Miguel put his hands in his pocket, thinking. "What about his bodyguard, Snake. I bet he's an ex con. He'll never make millions like Doctor Hyde. Maybe he wanted his boss out of the picture so he could take over. He killed Yu-Chen and framed his boss."

"To what purpose? So he can run Black Core Labs? Don't be ridiculous. The guy can't even talk in complete sentences."

"Maybe he just wants to blackmail his boss. Extortion. He offs Yu-Chen but tries to pin it on Hyde. Even if it never goes to trial, Hyde must be worried and want to keep Snake happy."

"If Snake crossed Hyde, he'd gamble his whole life," Amy said. "Only a rock-solid plan could make it worth it."

Several miles away, Snake rows a canoe on Lake Natoma. He checks the coast is clear. He digs into his pocket and pulls out Hyde's cufflink he picked up after it slipped off Hyde's wrist. The sapphire is missing. Snake drops Hyde's cufflink into the water. Rows on.

"There's one more person I can think of who could be a suspect. Officer White," said Miguel.

"Mike! Why would you think that?" asked Amy.

"I don't know. He sort of flaunts the law. He parks his SUV in the red zone a lot. I heard from the friend who is a law clerk. He told me a drunk driver got off scot-free. He was a friend of Mike's. Something about the breath results being lost.

At the empty police station, Mike stared at the screen that displayed the detective's notes on the rental car: witness statements, timelines, a slow parade of facts. White scrolled through the evidence until he found it: a photo of a sapphire bracelet, its largest stone missing. He hovered for a breath, then deleted the image, erasing the connection as cleanly as the click of a key. The net was tightening around him, but White had crossed too many lines to stop taking chances now.

Amy and Miguel walked side by side, neither willing to risk another debate. "It was a suicide, Miguel. We have to let it go," Amy said, her tone flat. Miguel swallowed his doubts, matching her pace as the noise of morning filled the park around them.

They kept moving, pressed by the certainty everyone expected, but a shared unease lingered behind their silence. It was a truth neither dared to touch. For now, both tried to believe the story was over.

Out on Folsom Boulevard, Paige steered the Impala toward Highway 50. The town faded in her mirrors, the first gold of morning pooling across her dashboard as she headed west. Sunlight streaked the sky and filled the car, carrying her farther from everything she'd left behind.

She slowed for a red light. A cyclist pulled alongside—Scott Lee. She'd seen him once or twice on her long runs, the quiet kid who spent more time in the hills than in town. He looked angular and awkward in slick spandex, his bike too new for someone who used to live for the trails. He glanced at her, uncertain, helmet low over his eyes.

"Paige?" His voice was soft, almost hesitant.

She rolled down the window, her jaw tight. "Hey, Scott. I didn't recognize you. Thought hiking was more your thing."

He shook his head, eyes down. "I stopped after... what happened up in Coloma last year."

She watched him, waiting. The pause stretched; Scott's hands fluttered nervously at the handlebars. He finally spoke, voice barely above a whisper. "I heard you're leaving town."

"Yeah." Paige's voice was flat. "Needed to."

Scott looked around, furtive, a quick dart of his eyes to the curb and back. "I'm sorry. Dad wanted to say goodbye. Um... I'm starting college next month."

She nodded, her skin prickling as Scott leaned in, words tumbling quieter than he meant: "It's good you're leaving. Sometimes... it's just better."

Across the street, a plain black sedan idled, tinted windows blank and unreadable. A pale hand flicked cigarette ash out the window, the gesture oddly deliberate. At the wheel sat Bao Ming, a midnight-blue HaoMao pack resting on the dash.

Scott glanced away just as fast, breath catching, as if afraid to focus too long or make direct eye contact. His pulse quickened, voice barely above a whisper. "Watch your back. There's always someone watching. Sometimes closer than you think."

Before Paige could answer, the light blinked green and the car behind her blared its horn. Scott jerked upright, pushed off, and sped down the bike lane without another word—his warning trailing after her like a shadow.

Paige stared at the books beside her. They felt heavier than she remembered, dense, like they carried more than words. She shook off the thought and eased onto the Highway 50 on-ramp, Scott Lee shrinking to a flicker in her rearview mirror—vanishing into sunlight and memory.

Neither she nor the world noticed the faint shimmer of gold dust along the books' spines.

Epilogue

Governor Gaffney sat at her desk, sunlight slanting across stacks of legislative briefings and yesterday's news.

Martin Beck entered the governor's office, his face drawn. "Governor, there's something you need to see." He set a thin folder on her desk. "I've just learned the men we let take custody of that Chinese miner's remains outside Folsom last year weren't real government agents. Their credentials were forgeries. Homeland only caught it now because of a database update on diplomatic IDs."

Governor Gaffney stared at him. "This was a year ago. Why am I just hearing about it now?"

"It slipped through because the forgeries were sophisticated, and the new alert system flagged them during a recent review," Beck replied. "If this gets out, it'll destroy our credibility ahead of the trade summit. And it could kill your shot at re-election."

She set her pen down, exhaling. "So, who the hell did we hand that body to?"

Beck hesitated, lowering his voice even more. "If this gets out, the press will eat us alive."

"You want to bury it?"

"A quiet internal review. We lock the file. No reason for Folsom PD or UC Davis to get dragged into an international incident. The last thing we need is to look like a bunch of rubes on the national stage."

Governor Gaffney's lips pressed into a thin line, eyes searching the window as if weighing the cost of silence. Finally, she nodded. "File it. Deep. No leaks, Marty."

He gave a tight smile and left. Alone in the polished stillness, Governor Gaffney rose from her chair and crossed to the window. She stared out at the city lights, her reflection hovering in the glass—a solitary keeper of a secret no one else would ever know.

As she turned away, the late sunlight slid across the glass, and for a brief moment, the room felt colder. Some secrets, she realized, were never really laid to rest.

***

Book 2 *Revenge of the Hungry Ghost:* When her murdered fiancé's ghost returns during the next Hungry Ghost Festival with a cryptic warning, former cop Paige Gold must hunt a stolen alchemist's treasure and unmask a deadly conspiracy before she becomes the next victim.

Continue the story in Book 2, coming summer 2026. Get updates on release dates, behind-the-scenes notes, and reader bonuses: sign up for my newsletter at CarynMcCann.com

Bonus Case File

For readers who like to dig deeper: download the police report that first made Jamal suspicious of his colleague, plus a Forensic Reader's Guide that walks you through every red flag, step by step.

Unlock the confidential police report: https://BookHip.com/GXP VVKVOr scan to access the suspicious case file.

Backstage Area

Acknowledgements

Deepest thanks to Lucija Dupljak, my insightful editor, and to Nabin Karna, whose artistry shines on the cover. And to every reader who embarks on this adventure. Your support is what lets stories reach the world.

Book club questions

1. Officer Paige Gold sees the museum heist as "small-town mischief," but then her view of her town and herself shifts. When did you first sense her worldview crack, and why?

2. Yu-Chen's gold-based "miracle cure" blends scientific hope with moral compromise. By the end, do you see him more as visionary, victim, or accomplice, and which choice fixed that view for you?

3. The museum heist, missing gold, and clashing reports create competing "truths." Which version—Paige's instincts, Hyde's story, the department's files, or the ghosts—did you trust most, and why?

4. The Hungry Ghost Festival and Mrs. Chen's beliefs give the story its supernatural lens on justice and grief. How did the ghostly encounters—especially with Charlie and Yu-Chen—change what you thought was really happening?

5. Several men—Hyde, White, David, even Paige's own department—try to steer her search for the truth. Where do you see genuine protection versus control, and how does that tension shape her final choices?

6. Imagine a truly independent police report on Yu-Chen's death. What single detail (time stamp, witness note, forensics result, missing evidence) would you most want clarified, and how might it alter the whole case?

7. The story blends East–West traditions, biotech greed, and an imperial secret about immortality. Which element hit you hardest—the ancient legend, the modern conspiracy, or Paige's losses—and why?

8. By the end, Paige has lost her badge, Yu-Chen, and faith in the system but not in the truth. If you wrote an epilogue set a year later, where would she be—inside and out—and what part of the case would still haunt her?

About the author

Caryn McCann is a screenwriter and novelist who blends international intrigue, emotional suspense, and cultural depth in her fiction. A former resident of Hong Kong, she studied Chinese language and culture at universities in Hong Kong and China. Her stories explore the intersection of justice and cultural traditions with a supernatural twist.

If you enjoyed this book, please leave a review on line. Your feedback means the world to me! Want behind-the-scenes intel, bonus scenes and news about upcoming releases?

Sign up for my newsletter at CarynMcCann.com for exclusive reveals and surprises!

www.ingramcontent.com/pod-product-compliance
Lightning Source LLC
LaVergne TN
LVHW091813110826
845146LV00006B/973

* 9 7 9 8 9 9 3 2 8 5 8 0 1 *